"God, you make me crazy. Do you know that?" Kay pushed Stef onto the rug in front of the fire. Passion for passion's sake. She unbuckled Stef's belt, pulled the woman's jeans down — slowly revealing curving hips, thighs, calves, ankles. Socks, sweater, underwear were thrown aside — finally exposing Stef's exquisite body. Kay stood and removed her own clothes, then knelt once again above Stef, mentally staggered by the rush, the heat that washed over her — just from looking. Not even touching. Yet.

Kay placed her hands over Stef's breasts and caressed them, rubbing her thumbs over the firm nipples. Stef pressed her thighs to Kay's hips and pulled Kay to her. Kay swallowed hard, overwhelmed that Stef had chosen to give herself so completely. Without whispered promises. Without the certainty of a next month or next year.

Shaken by the passion she felt — passion that had been buried for several years beneath the pain and unraveling of two lives — Kay made love to Stef almost guiltily, not knowing if the awakened passion would ever move her to do more than please Stef physically. Each touch, each stroke was done with tenderness, if not caring. Passion, if not love. But where did passion and love begin and end, Kay wondered. They seemed to wear the same disguise. As Stef shuddered with pleasure beneath her, the questions lingered.

About the Author

Love on the Line is Laura DeHart Young's third novel published by Naiad Press (the first was *There Will Be No Goodbyes* and the second was *Family Secrets*). She is currently at work on her fourth novel, *Private Passions*, which will be published by Naiad in 1998. Laura lives in Bethlehem, Pennsylvania.

Love
on the
Line

LAURA DeHart Young

THE NAIAD PRESS, INC.
1997

Printed in the United States of America on acid-free paper
First Edition

Editor: Christine Cassidy
Cover designer: Bonnie Liss (Phoenix Graphics)
Typesetter: Sandi Stancil

Library of Congress Cataloging-in-Publication Data

Young, Laura DeHart, 1956 –
    Love on the line / Laura DeHart Young.
        p.   cm.
    ISBN 1-56280-162-7 (p)
    I. Title.
PS3575.O799L68   1997
813'.54—dc21   96-45486
                                                                              CIP

For Lori and Gracie

Acknowledgments

All my love to Barb. Thanks for giving me the stars and for keeping the light on.

CHAPTER ONE

The helicopter approached Fairbanks from the north. From above, the land surrounding the city appeared flat — until a closer look revealed low rolling hills spreading out from the banks of the Chena River.

The helicopter banked and began its descent to the Fairbanks International Airport. Across clear skies to the south, Kay Westmore noted the snowcapped peaks called "three sisters." Mt. Hayes, Mt. Hess and Mt. Deborah rose like identical triplets into the heavens. As August faded into September the peaks were already beginning to winter. Cold, white, frozen. As all would be soon.

The helicopter landed gently. The sonorous rhythmic slashing of the blades vibrated through to her spine. Kay removed her helmet. The acrid smell of oil and fuel caused her to jump quickly from the passenger side of the cockpit. Bending low, she ran away from the long day into the blanketed peace of night.

Kay's associate and pilot, Russell Bend, escorted her to her car. "Better get some good sack time tonight, Kay. We've got that meeting tomorrow morning. Ten o'clock sharp."

"I'll be there, awake and alert." Kay smiled at the bear of a man. She and Russell had worked together for the past two years. He was like a brother — protective, playful, never far away when she needed him.

Russell ran his fingers through the patch of thick brown whiskers covering his face from lower cheek to chin. It was a stroke of thoughtfulness as much as speculation. "This meeting's gotta be something important. Donnelly's back from D.C. Hear he's brought some high-level guests."

Donnelly was Edward Donnelly, Regional Director, National Park Service, Alaska — the agency responsible for overseeing Alaska's more than 51 million acres of national park lands. It was the same agency Kay and Russell worked for — traveling eight months out of the year from park to park, assessing needs and problems.

"I've heard rumors of a joint project with the Forest Service in Yukon Flats," Kay said.

"Could be why we're meeting." Russell's large

six-foot frame lumbered toward his old Ford pickup. He smiled and waved. "Remember to be civilized tomorrow, Kay! No farting, burping or scratching."

She laughed. "I'll try my best!"

"They're right to keep folks like you and me confined to wilderness areas. Civilization is so bourgeois."

Kay laughed again and waved. Stepping up to her Honda Passport, she groaned softly. Tired. She'd stop for one or two beers then head home.

The small dance club glistened neon pastels — pink, blue, lavender. The long oak-wood bar was full, but Kay managed to squeeze into the far left corner. Ten minutes later, cold beer in hand, she stood alongside the dance floor. Swaying to the music, Kay watched no one in particular.

"Hiya, Kay."

Kay looked up. It was Stef. She reached up and offered Kay a hug. Kay accepted the human contact, putting her arm around Stef's back. "How are you?"

"Great." Stef took Kay's hand and frowned. "Called you the other night. No answer."

Stef was obviously disappointed. "Been traveling."

"There're some tables in the back. Want to sit? You look kinda tired."

"Okay. Actually, it's been a long day."

Kay followed Stef into the adjoining game room. Just beyond the pinball and video machines were some tables in a low-lit area near the kitchen. The smell of fried food permeated the room. Some of the tables had been pushed together to accommodate a

3

large group of women celebrating someone's birthday. Candles were being extinguished amidst cheering and clapping.

Stef sat down at the table farthest from the crowd, her long shapely legs dangling over the side of the chair. A very short skirt revealed perfectly sculptured thighs. Kay blinked. She'd been in the wilderness too long.

Stef's sun-blond hair bounced luxuriously over her shoulders. Even in the shadows her green eyes shone like glow-in-the-dark paints. "Saw you here last week."

Kay smiled. "Last Monday. The day before I left for my week-long jaunt. You should've said hello."

"You were with other people. How come you're alone tonight?"

"Just got back a half-hour ago. You're the first person I've seen." Kay studied the young woman's face — perfect pink-blush skin, cute ski-jump nose, beautiful smile. She'd met Stef Kramer six or seven times within the last few months, enjoying many buoyant conversations and, admittedly, the attention Stef seemed eager to give. A mutual friend had introduced them at a party near the river earlier that spring. Kay and Stef had talked for hours on a bank of grass beneath a towering spruce tree, listening to the water flow as easily as their conversation.

"Have you thought about me, Kay?"

Kay didn't have to lie. "Yes, I have." But there were complications in her life and she was reluctant to involve Stef — as intriguing as she was. And, of course, there was the age problem.

Stef reached across the table and rested her hands on Kay's. "You look fantastic."

4

Kay tried to swallow the golf-ball-sized lump in her throat. "Thanks. That was nice of you to say."

Her lips protruded slightly into a pout. "Why haven't you called?"

Kay intertwined her fingers with Stef's. "Like I said, I've been away. And, we've talked about this before. I suspect I'm a bit too old for you."

"I adore older women. Most people my age are dull and boring." Stef smiled disarmingly.

Kay leaned forward. "How old do you adore them? I'm thirty-eight."

"Kay, we're perfect for each other! I just turned twenty-two in January. Let's dance."

Kay sighed and got up. Her legs felt like rubber as Stef slipped an arm through hers. "I suppose one dance can't hurt."

Stef smiled again. "Don't count on it."

The young woman's curves fit into Kay's as though the two of them had been parted at birth. The warmth was not unwelcome. Kay's travels from one side of the state to the other left little time for romance.

Stef's head rested on Kay's shoulder. Her hair was fragrant and baby soft. But she was a baby. What am I doing, Kay thought.

Stef wrapped her arms securely around Kay's neck. Looking directly into her eyes she asked, "Where were you, darling?"

The word *darling* threw Kay off-balance. "Pardon?"

"You said you just got back from a trip."

"Gates of the Arctic. National preserve up north. Ever been there?"

"No. Will you take me?"

Kay laughed. "Maybe."

"I'd keep you warm."

"No doubt."

"Being a forest ranger, you must know all the nifty spots. Romantic. Private."

"A few. Still at the university?"

"Yep. Full-time now. My education grant finally happened so I cut back my hours at the Alumni Office to part-time. With the grant, and a little help from Daddy, I'm in pretty good shape."

Kay ran her hands along Stef's sides, stopping at her hips. "Yes, you certainly are."

Stef giggled softly, flicking Kay's right earlobe with her tongue. "Thank you."

Stepping back, Kay tried to compose herself. "Well, we better sit down and finish our beers. Can't make this a late night. Important meeting tomorrow."

Stef grabbed Kay's arms. "This is an important meeting too, Kay. I know we've met before — but this time's special. I can feel it."

She took Kay's hands and leaned upward, her soft mouth finding Kay's, gently biting Kay's lower lip.

Kay drifted away — from the music, the room, the hour. She was locked on Stef's lips, sensuously parting her own, on the tongue that slipped inside her mouth. No. This couldn't be happening now. This mustn't happen now.

Kay ended the kiss. "Think we better sit down."

Stef followed her back to the table. "Didn't you like the dance, Kay?"

"I liked it." A little too much, Kay thought.

Stef volunteered to get two more beers. Kay was relieved for the time to regroup. What did Stef want with her, she wondered. She felt strangely weakened by the attention. Vulnerable.

"Well, Kay. Fancy meeting you here."

The all-too-familiar voice cut like a machete into her quiet reflection. She looked up, resigned to the presence even before sight made it official. "Barbara. What brings you out tonight? Full moon?"

"Kay, I'm so glad you haven't lost your sense of humor. It's so damned endearing."

Kay glared at her former lover, heart sagging with the effort it took to communicate with this person. Barbara was dressed immaculately in neatly pressed navy blue slacks, white cotton shirt and gray sweater vest. As usual, not a stitch out of place. "Please, not tonight. Go have a drink. Meet some new people. Have fun."

"You'd like that, I'm sure. Anything to be rid of me."

"I tried the friendship thing, Barb. It didn't work."

Her face softened into cavities of pain. "I've no interest in being friends, Kay. I want you back in my life. Back in my bed. I love you."

Eleven months had passed since their break-up. After five years together, the relationship had ultimately twisted and turned into suffocation for Kay. Barb's jealousy and possessiveness had choked her off from friends, family — from herself. She had somehow come to be lost in an existence of Barb's choosing. The break-up went badly for both of them. Barb refused to let go. Lately, there had been phone calls in the middle of the night. Hang-ups. Odd notes

7

in the mail. Typed. Unsigned. Kay suspected Barb but chose not to confront her, hoping she'd grow bored. Find someone new.

"Please, Barb. As I said, not tonight. I'm really beat. Okay?"

"Can't we even get together and talk?"

"About what? What topic is there that we haven't already covered concerning the end of our relationship?"

"Here's your beer, Kay." Stef set the frosted mug on the table. Turning toward Barb, Stef introduced herself. "Hiya. I'm Stef. You a friend of Kay's?"

Barb smirked, obviously amused by the question. "You could say that. Barbara Reynolds." Barb glared at Kay with transparent disdain. "You didn't tell me you had a date."

"Stef is a friend I just happened to run into tonight."

Stef pointed toward the empty chair across from Kay. "Grab a seat, Barbara. Join us."

Barb sat down. "Thanks. Kay and I weren't finished talking yet." She took a napkin and wiped the table down to her own satisfaction.

"On the contrary, Barb was just leaving," Kay said. Taking Stef's hand, she squeezed it. "Thanks for the beer. You sit down."

As Kay was about to get up, Stef plopped herself into Kay's lap. "I can sit here, Kay. That way your friend can talk with us for a while."

Kay avoided Barb's stare, utterly afraid of those dagger eyes — eyes that could pierce titanium steel. Beads of sweat trickled down the nape of her neck as Stef continued to blunder on, oblivious of the situation.

8

"Kay and I met at a party this spring." Stef flipped some stray hair away from Kay's eyes. "I was attracted to her right away. She was so easy to talk to. Great sense of humor. Beautiful blue eyes."

"Yes, Kay can be quite charming when she wants to be," Barb said with a callous sneer.

Stef smiled sweetly and hugged Kay. "Kay's a great kisser, too. Found that out tonight."

"I've had quite enough of this!" Red-faced, Barb got up and kicked the wooden chair into the table. Drinks spilled from one end to the other. "Picking them a little young, aren't you, Kay? Been hanging out at the elementary school?"

"Barb, for God's sake . . ."

"Well, you and your little whore can fuck right here and now for all I care." Barb kicked the wooden chair once more. "This isn't over yet, Kay. I'll get you back — one way or another."

And then she was suddenly gone. Kay was stunned, speechless. Stef had tears in her eyes. Kay hugged her tightly. "I'm so sorry that happened."

Stef kissed Kay's cheek, fingers running softly through Kay's dark hair. "Who was she? She was horrible."

Kay sighed. "She wasn't always so horrible. Barb and I were lovers for five years. We broke up about a year ago. Two days after my birthday." Inside, emotions ripped at her stomach.

"Now I'm the one who's sorry. I didn't mean to make her mad. I thought she was just a friend."

"You didn't do anything wrong." Kay got up, lifting Stef from the chair with her. Setting her down, Kay said quietly, "Time to go. This party's unfortunately over."

"You're not going to leave me here are you?"

Kay put her hands on either side of Stef's face. "Listen to me. You're beautiful and sweet. I'm utterly flattered that you like me. But I'm too old for you."

Stef crossed her arms in front of her chest. "Everyone thinks they know what's best for me. Can you at least give me a ride back to campus? A friend of mine dropped me off here."

Kay grabbed her hand. "I'm sorry. Of course I can give you a ride."

The moon was full, the night air cold. They rode in silence. Kay took Philips Field Road to University Avenue.

"Where's your dorm, hon?" Kay asked.

"Hang a right here. Two blocks down on the left."

Kay stopped in front of a three-story stone building. "This it?"

"Yeah. 'Night, Kay."

"Goodnight."

Stef leaned over and kissed her softly on the lips. "Hope I see you soon."

"You will."

Kay watched and waited as Stef disappeared into the building's side entrance. Just as she was ready to drive away, Stef returned — face pressed up against the passenger window. Kay reached over and rolled it down.

"Something wrong?"

"Shit, Kay. My roommate's entertaining a friend."

She rolled her eyes. "Not a good time to bust in on her, if you know what I mean."

Kay shook her head back and forth. Slightly annoyed, she said, "Get in. You can stay at my place for the night."

Stef grinned. "Thanks, Kay."

"I've got an extra room. That's where you'll sleep."

Stef shrugged. "I can think of better arrangements."

"I'm sure you can."

In the guest room of her three-bedroom apartment, Kay flipped the light switch on. "Think you'll be comfortable in here. There's an extra toothbrush in the bathroom cabinet. And there're some extra sweats — whatever you want to sleep in — in the hallway dresser. Help yourself."

"I usually sleep in the nude."

Kay ignored the flutter in her stomach. "In that case, you're all set. Goodnight."

In the darkness Kay drifted just short of sleep, thinking about Stef down the hall. Thinking about Barb and the painful scene at the club. How long was Barb's anger going to last, festering like an open wound? It wasn't as though their relationship had been perfect. Barb had strayed several times, but she always came back, holding on tighter than before.

More controlling. More determined to keep Kay to herself — away from parties, away from family events, away from life. They did everything together or nothing at all. And while Barb had her solitary forays out into the world, Kay stayed home. Cleaned. Cooked. Worked. Work had been her only escape. And jogging.

One day Kay had jogged along the Chena River. She often ran two or three miles. But that day she jogged five . . . six . . . seven. By the time she got home she was much later than usual. Barb was waiting for her at the top of the front porch steps. Arms crossed in front of her. Anger leaping from her eyes.

"Where've you been?"

"Running."

"You're late."

Kay shrugged. "I went farther than I usually do."

"Liar."

"Barb, for Christ's sake! Will you look at me? I just jogged seven fucking miles. Now get out of my way."

Barb stood firm, blocking Kay's way inside the building. "Who is she?"

"Who's who?"

"The bitch you're fucking behind my back. That's goddamned who!"

"You're crazy. Get out of my way."

"Why are you doing this to me, Kay? I love you."

"I'm not doing anything, Barb. You won't let me do anything. And it's killing our relationship. Don't you see that?"

"I only see you're trying to dump me."

"No. I'm trying to run away from you, but I can't seem to run far enough. Five miles. Ten miles. A thousand fucking miles! It doesn't matter. It'll never be far enough."

She had pushed by Barb, running up the stairs into the apartment. Running away. The voice behind her was always there. "I'll never let you go, Kay. Never."

Kay rolled over, curling up against the memory. So far, Barb had kept her promise. She wasn't letting go. A sudden burst of cool air hit Kay's back . . . then a welcome warmth, arms gently clasped around her stomach.

"It's freezing in that room," Stef said. "I could croak in there."

Kay chuckled. "Sorry. I usually keep that room closed off. No need to waste heat."

"You're not going to send me back to that frozen tundra, are you?" Stef asked hopefully.

"No. You may stay."

"Thanks."

"But you must behave."

"Of course." Stef nuzzled against Kay's neck.

Kay closed her eyes — hoping for instantaneous sleep. But that was like hoping for long winter days. There was movement behind her. Suddenly, Stef's lovely thighs were straddling Kay's stomach. She kissed Kay's forehead, cheeks, mouth. Kay's shirt was lifted above her head. Lips continued to kiss her, moving down Kay's chin, along her neck to her chest, Stef's mouth lingering at her nipples. Her tongue slid across each one, sending Kay's thoughts far away from the ticking clock — as if the passage of time ever mattered at moments like this. The mouth continued its work, pressing Kay into what she fondly referred to as the "sensual dimension." It was a crossing over she hadn't made in many months.

Stef rose slightly, took Kay's hand and drew it in between her legs. Kay felt herself slip inside. She followed Stef's rocking movements, her free hand caressing Stef's breasts.

"I've wanted you ever since the river," Stef whispered, staring straight into Kay's eyes. "I wanted you to have me."

Kay leaned upward, kissing Stef gently — but with enough force to consecrate their actions.

"Hold me, Kay. I want to come in your arms."

Kay rolled her over, hand still pumping inside. Stef put her arms around Kay's neck and stared into her eyes. She shuddered, moaned, then shuddered again.

Stef pushed Kay onto her back. Opening Kay's thighs, she slowly stroked Kay with her tongue.

Kay's head swam with pleasure — with confusion. She hadn't wanted any of this. Really. Passion, tenderness, complications. The orgasm came and pulsed away. She pulled Stef into her arms and held her there, caressed her, kissed her. Not wanting to hold on, not wanting to let go.

Kay woke to the grayness of morning. Her first thoughts belonged to Stef. She looked down to find Stef's arm draped across her waist. Stroking Stef's hair, she kissed her forehead, pulled her closer. She noticed the lightly freckled skin atop Stef's shoulders;

the curve of breasts not seen in the darkness; the soft, pink lips Kay had kissed again and again, stopping only when the moments had regrettably run down into sleep.

Stef stirred. Kay smiled and kissed the bridge between Stef's two gray-green eyes, eyes the color of tree bark moss. "Morning, beautiful."

Stretching her arms upward, Stef yawned. "Kay, I'm really here with you. Thought it was a dream."

Kay turned over. "Then it was a wonderful dream."

"How would you like to get away for the weekend?" Stef kissed Kay's fingertips. "My parents have a cabin near the mountains and Chatinika. It's kinda rustic. Definitely your style."

"We could go this weekend?"

"No one's using it right now."

"Looking forward to a weekend with you may actually get me through this day."

CHAPTER TWO

Just after ten Kay opened the door to a large conference room on the fourth floor of the National Park Service building located in downtown Fairbanks. As she entered the room all heads swung toward her. Many pairs of eyes seemed to guide her toward the empty seat nearest Russell Bend.

"Good morning," Kay said as cheerily as possible. "Please excuse my lateness." And then she lied. "Some unexpected car trouble."

Russell leaned over and whispered to Kay

underneath his breath. "You look like shit. What the hell happened?"

Kay forced a smile as she whispered back, "Long story."

Pushing his glasses forward from the bridge of his nose, Edward Donnelly glanced at her. His white hair and cobalt blue eyes contrasted with his coal-black suit. "So glad you could join us, Kay. Hope we didn't keep you from more important matters."

Kay shifted in her chair. "Not at all, Ed."

"Good. Then let me make some quick introductions." Donnelly swiveled his chair to the left, extending his right arm to the gentleman seated next to him. "This is Charles Eagleton, Acting Secretary of the Interior. Charles, Kay Westmore."

Kay nodded and smiled as Eagleton rose slightly from his chair, reaching out to shake her hand. "Pleasure meeting you, sir." Kay had heard a great deal about this man — a staunch environmentalist with close ties to the Vice President. The Secretary of the Interior post was currently vacant. Eagleton was the presumed successor to Thomas Evans, the former Secretary, who had resigned several weeks ago because of poor health.

"Let me also introduce Ted Mitchell of the Attorney General's office," Donnelly continued. "Ted represents the Attorney General directly on the project we're about to discuss. Also, Grace Perry of the Interior Office. Ms. Perry is in charge of the environmental compliance division."

Kay shook hands all around. Clearing his throat, Donnelly explained the purpose of the meeting. "The Department of the Interior and the Attorney General have requested our help in a joint project with the National Park Service of Alaska." He got up and walked to the room's far wall where he unveiled a state map that dramatically illustrated the 800-mile route of the Alaska Pipeline. "The project, as you can probably guess, involves the pipeline. When construction of the pipeline began in nineteen seventy-five a stringent quality assurance program was written into the construction agreement between the eight controlling oil companies and the state of Alaska. In addition to rigorous construction standards, this quality assurance program included continual visual inspection of the line, one hundred percent weld checks and other safety inspections. As a result, expected years of service for the pipeline was estimated at twenty-five years."

Kay nodded. This was common industry knowledge, although she guessed that most of the American public didn't know it.

Donnelly came back to the table, resting his hands on his chair. "Evidence has been obtained by the office of the Interior that these stringent quality assurance measures have been lax in recent years."

"Ed, let me break in here," Eagleton offered. The tall, youthful man stood and approached the map, his hands buried in both trouser pockets. "The Department of the Interior is committed to providing the environmental stewardship Alaskan voters expected when the pipeline was first built. More than twenty years have passed and the pipeline is aging. There are disturbing reports of sloppy inspections, improper weld checks and oil leaks of up to fifteen thousand barrels per leak. The oil companies are being less than cooperative. The Attorney General has been informed and, as a result, has agreed that a complete investigation is necessary."

Kay grimaced. The oil-stained legacy left by the *Exxon Valdez* disaster in 1989 was still burnt into her consciousness. It was an accident caused by arrogance and negligence, resulting in the Oil Pollution Act of 1990 — an act that imposed tougher civil and criminal penalties on oil companies responsible for negligent spills. And rightly so, Kay thought. The *Exxon Valdez,* while impaled on Bligh Reef in Prince William Sound, hemorrhaged more than 40,000 tons of oil over 10,000 square miles. Twelve hundred miles of Alaskan coastline, including the shores of three of the national parks Kay worked in, became oil-slicked horrors overnight. More than half a million birds and 6,000 marine mammals were killed, the largest known mortality of birds and marine mammals in any oil-related disaster. Kay had held many of those animals in her arms as they died.

Donnelly turned to Grace Perry. "Grace, perhaps you'd like to explain how the investigation will be conducted."

"Certainly," she replied.

Kay watched the dark-haired woman approach the map. She wore a simple royal-blue knit suit accented by a gold necklace. Her fair complexion, hourglass figure and long shapely legs gave her an aura of regality that seemed out of place in this Fairbanks conference room.

"Gentlemen," Grace Perry began, "and woman," she nodded toward Kay, "as you probably know, the Alaska pipeline stretches for eight hundred miles from the pumping stations at Prudhoe Bay to the storage tanks at Valdez." She indicated the pipeline's path on the map behind her. "Interior proposes an impromptu inspection beginning in mid-October. The regular Interior inspection isn't scheduled to take place until next spring. So, we'll have some element of surprise — at least for the first few days. By the time the oil companies are aware of our presence, everything will be set in motion." She turned toward the group. "It's up North where the most disturbing reports have originated concerning spills. We'll have a split team. One third of our team will inspect the pipeline from Fairbanks south to Valdez. Two-thirds of our team will inspect Fairbanks north to Prudhoe Bay. The operation will include visual and internal inspections, as well as weld X-rays."

"That's where Kay and Russell come in," Donnelly interjected.

Grace Perry nodded in agreement. "Correct, Ed. I need people familiar with the northern portion of the state — every inch of it — to help us with that leg of the inspection. The northern route is the longest and most difficult. I'll personally be in charge of that operation. The southern route will be handled by an associate of mine and other personnel from your department."

"We'll end up with a comprehensive report and supporting data to be reviewed by the Attorney General and, if necessary, the President," Mitchell said. His face suddenly crinkled into a mass of worry lines. "What we're really talking about here is our national security. The pipeline supports two million barrels of oil per day. Any major disruption in the flow of that oil and our national security could be dangerously compromised."

Grace opened a box at the far end of the table. From it she grabbed a stack of bound papers. "The reports I'm distributing explain our objectives in more detail and how we plan to meet them. It also explains what information, supplies and assistance we'll need from Miss Westmore and Mr. Bend. Study your copies and return them to Ed."

Russell Bend raised the sandwich to his mouth, then stopped. "You're still getting those letters and phantom phone calls?"

"Yes."

"Still think it's Barb?"

Kay shook her head. "Don't know what else to think, Russ. She was really angry at the bar last night."

Russ took a bite of his sandwich. A drop of mayonnaise ran into his beard. "I liked Barb. You two made a nice couple till she went screwy. Now she's a couple cards shy of a deck."

"Maybe so."

"But you've met someone new. Tell me about her."

The thought of Stef made Kay smile. "I met Stef about five months ago at a party. Since then we've seen each other a few times." Images of the previous night flashed through her mind like a vividly remembered dream. "Last night just sort of happened."

Sitting back in his chair, Russell stared at her for several moments. He positioned his hands like a picture frame in front of Kay's face. "You look a bit tired . . . but you do have this glow about you. Looks nice."

"A man with sensitivity. God, what a gem. No wonder your wife's hung on to you for ten years."

"Well, there're all kinds of stereotypes, Kay. Don't have to tell you that. So, now and then, I try to break a mold or two."

Kay poked at her salad, digging through the lettuce to see if anything interesting remained. "So, what do you think of the pipeline investigation?"

"Well, they picked a helluva time of year for it. The weather's gonna be nutso. But, nobody asked our opinion — even if we are supposed to be the goddamned experts."

"What if there are structural problems?"

Russ pushed his empty plate away. "This is politics, Kay. Somebody's bucking for a political appointment, if you ask me."

"Donnelly?"

"Who knows? Probably the whole lot of them."

"Why do I think it's all being done at our expense, Russ? This isn't a walk in the park we're talking about."

"Listen, Donnelly's probably having a fancy suit tailored for himself as we speak. For his trip to the Oval Office."

"Should I buy a dress? I don't even own one."

"Yeah. When I rent my tux — which shouldn't be any time soon."

Alex Chambers, Kay's oldest and dearest friend,

sat in the corner booth nursing a beer. Her gray sweatshirt had been fashionably altered. Turned inside out and missing its collar, the garment fell off her shoulders — creamy skin a contrast against the dark-paneled wall behind her.

"Where's Pat?" Kay asked as she and Stef approached.

Alex rolled her eyes. "She's addicted to one of the pinball machines." She got up and kissed Kay on the cheek, then turned toward Stef. "Hi. Alex Chambers, pinball widow."

Stef smiled as they sat down. "Hiya. Stef Kramer."

"Kay's told me a lot about you, Stef. Didn't you two meet at the river party this spring?"

"Uh huh. My eye's been on Kay ever since."

"From the look in your eyes now, it seems like your patience finally paid off."

Stef took Kay's hand. "Hope so."

Alex ran her index finger through the condensation on her beer glass. "Well, when the pinball wizard finally returns you'll meet Pat. We've been together seven years."

"Gosh, that's really wonderful," Stef said. "You must love each other very much."

Kay put her arm around Stef's shoulder. "Alex and Pat make a great couple. And you couldn't find two better friends anywhere."

"I'll round up some drinks," Stef offered. "Want anything, Alex?"

"Another beer would be super. Thanks."

Kay and Alex sat for a few moments in silence. Finally Kay said, "You're looking a bit glum. What's up?"

"Nothing new. Just one of those days."

"You two aren't fighting, are you?"

"No. I'm just being paranoid as usual. You know Pat. She's so independent it scares me sometimes."

"Not everyone basks in domesticity like you, Al."

"I know. But forget all that. Tell me about Stef."

"What's to tell? She's terrific."

"She's downright gorgeous." Alex shook her head. "God."

"She's lovely. Sweet. Innocent. I feel so . . ."

Alex looked confused. "What?"

Kay stared down at the table. "Oh, I don't know."

Alex laughed. "Lucky? Kay, she absolutely adores you. I just saw the way she looked at you — and it's not a look of innocence, I might add. She wants you, honey."

"She's had me."

"Oh," Alex said, smiling. "Does this mean you're official newlyweds?"

"I wouldn't say that. I'm very unsure of this whole thing. I feel . . . guilty."

"Guilty?"

"Because I let things get out of hand." Kay slapped her hands on the table in frustration. "I can't deal with any commitments right now. Barb's still up to her old tricks and, hell, it's been so long I don't know what I'm doing."

"Hey, honey, put the brakes on here. Relax. Have fun."

"You know me, Al. I'm slow at this sort of stuff." Kay looked around at the crowd of people, then lowered her voice. "I'm not into using people — or sleeping around, for that matter."

"I think you're being hard on yourself. Give

24

things some time. You may end up as lovesick as Stef."

"Looky who I found."

Alex and Kay glanced up. It was Stef, with Pat in tow. Pat's face was all grin — like she'd just won the million-dollar lottery.

"And I thought I was shit out of luck," Pat blurted. "Next thing you know, this lovely young lady's standing next to me giving me the eye. She made me lose my game."

Alex laughed. "Well, that's a first."

Pat slid in next to Alex. "Not true. First time I ever saw you, honey, was during a game of video poker. Missed a royal flush because of you."

Alex shook her head. "Funny. I don't remember that."

"As soon as I saw her I knew it was Pat," Stef said. "She looked like a professional."

Pat leaned forward and grabbed Kay's shoulder. "Hey, Kay. I gotta tell you — guess who I saw this afternoon at the supermarket."

"Who?"

"Barb."

Kay winced. "Lovely."

Pat took several gulps of her beer. "Would you believe she shot me the finger?"

"You're joking," Kay said.

"No way. All I did was wave and say hi from the opposite end of cereal aisle."

Kay rolled her eyes. "You should've been here for the scene she caused the other night. It was pretty awful."

"Tell them what happened," Stef said.

Kay explained about the fight at the bar, the

anonymous letters and the strange phone calls. Alex and Pat stared in amazement.

"I'm meeting with a detective. Things are getting out of hand."

"When?" Alex asked, her voice shaken with concern.

"Monday."

Kay put the luggage into the back seat of the Passport. Stef was still inside gathering the last of the food supply. She repositioned the luggage until she was satisfied. A voice from behind startled her.

"Hey beautiful. Going away again?"

Kay turned to find her next-door neighbor, Carl Hall, standing alongside the curb. He was holding a broom. Carl was always holding a broom, a shovel, an ice pick — depending on the time of year. It was how he kept abreast of other people's comings and goings.

"Hey, Carl. Yes. Heading North for the weekend."

"Where to?"

"A cabin my friend has near Chatinika. Near Beaver Creek."

Carl smiled and switched the broom handle from one hand to the other. "Oh, that's a nice spot. One of my friends has a cabin near the creek. Every now and then we go hunting and fishing up there. You'll love it."

"Weather's supposed to be nice this weekend. Clear and cool."

Nodding, Carl's blue eyes seemed to shift continuously from Kay to the car and back to Kay. Carl was an attractive man in his late fifties, Kay guessed. He was a bit of a health nut and kept himself in excellent physical condition. He liked to run and sometimes Kay jogged with him. Kay felt sorry for him. He'd moved into the apartment building two years ago after his wife died. He'd worshipped his wife. Whenever he talked about her, the loneliness was painfully obvious.

"You have a new friend I see," Carl said.

"Yes. Her name's Stef."

Carl backed away from the street, broom straw sweeping over the pavement in front of him. "Well, I know what it's like to be lonely. Have a nice trip, Kay."

"Thanks. I will."

The two-lane road to Chatinika was called Steese Highway. It curved languidly along the southern base of the White Mountains, an unobtrusive path leading from city to wilderness.

"How long have your parents owned the cabin?"

Stef rested her head on Kay's shoulder, hands clasped around Kay's upper arm. "About ten years. It's a beautiful setting. You'll love it."

"Your parents use the place much?"

"Mostly Daddy. He and his buddies use the cabin during the summer. But he hardly goes up past August. Just closes the place for the winter. Mom gave me a set of keys in case I wanted to take some school friends."

"Something tells me your mother wouldn't approve of the guest you've chosen. I'm not exactly a school pal."

"Actually, my parents know about me. And they're pretty cool with it. Maybe you'll get to meet them."

"Where do they live?"

"In Nenana." She reached up and kissed Kay's cheek. "Don't worry. We'll be alone this weekend. I wouldn't subject you to a meeting with my parents just yet."

"Thanks."

The cabin was chilly inside. Kay immediately searched for firewood while Stef unloaded the car. About an hour later, in front of a roaring fire, they sat in the living room roasting hot-dogs.

"Shit. I burnt mine, Kay."

A charred hot-dog hung precariously at the end of a stick. "Doesn't look too appetizing," Kay said, glancing at the oversized sweater that teasingly bared Stef's shoulder. "You, on the other hand, look absolutely delicious." She kissed the top of Stef's shoulder, lingering over her lightly perfumed skin.

"Well, I wasn't hungry anyway. At least not for this." Stef straddled Kay's lap and placed her hands on either side of Kay's face. "Make love to me, Kay. All weekend long."

Kay closed her eyes as Stef kissed her. She tried to ignore the tickle in the pit of her stomach. The attraction she felt for Stef was strong — stronger than any physical attraction she'd ever known. But that's all it was, she told herself. Physical. Sensual. Nothing more. Mentally, she blocked emotion. There would be no hurt. No long, drawn-out process of love's highs and lows. Not for this young woman. Not for her.

"God, you make me crazy. Do you know that?" Kay pushed Stef onto the rug in front of the fire. Passion for passion's sake. She unbuckled Stef's belt, pulled the woman's jeans down — slowly revealing curving hips, thighs, calves, ankles. Socks, sweater, underwear were thrown aside — finally exposing Stef's exquisite body. Kay stood and removed her own clothes, then knelt once again above Stef, mentally staggered by the rush, the heat that washed over her — just from looking. Not even touching. Yet.

Kay placed her hands over Stef's breasts and caressed them, rubbing her thumbs over the firm nipples. Stef pressed her thighs to Kay's hips and pulled Kay to her. Kay swallowed hard, overwhelmed that Stef had chosen to give herself so completely. Without whispered promises. Without the certainty of a next month or next year.

Shaken by the passion she felt — passion that had been buried for several years beneath the pain and unraveling of two lives — Kay made love to Stef almost guiltily, not knowing if the awakened passion would ever move her to do more than please Stef physically. Each touch, each stroke was done with tenderness, if not caring. Passion, if not love. But where did passion and love begin and end, Kay wondered. They seemed to wear the same disguise. As Stef shuddered with pleasure beneath her, the questions lingered.

Stef coaxed Kay upward, kissing her, pulling Kay on top of her. "I want you inside me." Stef guided her hand, holding onto Kay's shoulders. "I never thought, in my whole life, it'd be like this."

29

Kay's inner turmoil continued as she watched the tears drop from Stef's eyes. She bent down and kissed them away, her hand continuing. She could feel Stef's muscles tighten. Stef sighed and closed her eyes. Moments passed in silence as they lay in each other's arms.

"It's like touching the stars." Stef lay her head on Kay's chest. "Coming with you inside me."

"Then we'll travel the entire universe together."

"Doing the stars."

Kay cleared her throat, struggling to compose herself. "Yes. Doing the stars."

The next morning, the two women walked hand-in-hand through the mist along Beaver Creek. They'd followed the creek for a mile or more until it turned sharply to the west, its eastern banks paralleling the edge of a clearing. Through the last stretch of forest pines, the clearing of high golden grasses suddenly shimmered with the first light of day. And in the distance, somewhere near the middle of that vast space, a herd of caribou wandered into view, lazily but alertly grazing in the bordering scrub.

Kay stooped and pointed. "Look, Stef. Aren't they beautiful?"

"Gosh, look at them. But you must see all kinds of wildlife." Stef sat down on a rock near the edge of the creek. Kay was still hunched over, facing the herd, her back toward Stef. "I've hardly ever left Fairbanks."

Kay continued to watch the animals, Stef's comment lost amidst her own thoughts.

Playfully, Stef extended her right leg and kicked Kay in the back end. Kay lost her balance and toppled gracelessly onto the forest floor.

"Hey, what's the big idea?" Kay asked, raking leafy debris from her hair.

"You were ignoring me," Stef said with a coy smile. "I don't like to be ignored, lover." She laughed. "Your bedtime pleasures might be revoked."

"Oh, really?" Kay got up and grabbed Stef around the waist. "We'll see about that." She pulled Stef onto the ground and they rolled across the moist earth. Kay tried to shove a handful of pine needles down Stef's back.

"Kay!" Stef complained, trying to dig down her back for the prickly needles. "They're all wet."

Kay ended up on top of Stef, running her hands through the soft blond hair and occasional pine needle. The sight of the young woman's face, red-cheeked and glowing, pierced Kay's heart suddenly, without warning. "I think I'm very glad you found me," she said. Softly and delicately she bit the outer edges of Stef's lips. "Do I get my bedtime privileges back?"

Stef grinned, her green eyes deepening in color as they reflected the overhead pines. "I could never say no to you."

"I'm happy to hear it."

"What's the most beautiful thing you've seen, Kay?"

"In Alaska?"

"Yes."

"You."

"Let's go back inside."

CHAPTER THREE

For fifteen minutes Kay had been waiting patiently in the Fairbanks Police Department lobby. Finally, a young man in his mid-thirties walked out from a nearby corridor. He was dressed in a navy blue suit, pale blue shirt and multicolored tie that reminded her of a Van Gogh painting until she realized, upon closer inspection, that it was a Van Gogh painting.

"Miss Westmore?" he asked, blond curls falling

33

across his forehead, his hand stroking *Starry, Starry Night.*

"You must be Detective Meadows."

"In the flesh."

He escorted Kay into a small shared office where two other detectives were working, one talking on the phone, the other squinting at a computer screen.

"Have a seat, Miss Westmore."

Kay sat down on the same type of wooden chair she'd been sitting on earlier. Her ass was feeling flatter than a newly paved road. "Have you looked at the information I sent you?"

"Yeah. I've got the details here in a report." The detective rifled through the papers on his desk. A few landed on the floor. "Somewhere." More papers were shoved. "Tell you what, Miss Westmore . . . uh, Kay. Can I call you Kay?"

"Fine."

"Kay, why don't we just talk? The clerk is probably typing the report as we speak. Where do you live?"

"Mount View Drive."

"Really?" He smiled like a used-car salesman. "I live on Summit Road. Guess that makes us practically neighbors."

"Sort of."

"Live alone?"

"Yes."

"So do I. How 'bout that? Something else we have in common." The detective looked at his watch. "Know what, Kay? It's after five. Why don't we have dinner? You can tell me all about your problem in a nice, pleasant atmosphere."

34

Kay sighed. This guy was an idiot, no doubt about it. "Detective Meadows —"

"Bob. Call me Bob. Please."

"Okay, Bob. Did you even look at the information I sent you?"

"Well, actually I only glanced at it briefly. But, from what I gather, it appears someone is stalking you." He leaned back in his chair, arms folded on top of his one-track mind. "Of course, meeting you in person and seeing how attractive you are, it doesn't surprise me."

Kay smiled to herself. In a way, this was going to be fun. "Well, just to refresh your memory, I've been getting letters. Typewritten and unsigned. Copies which I sent you last week." Kay crossed her legs. Bob's eyes followed their movement. "I've also been getting phone calls in the middle of the night. Hang-ups. This has been going on for months and, quite frankly, I've had it."

The detective let out a slow, high-pitched whistle. "I understand completely, Kay. Tell you what. I'll track down that information and we'll continue this discussion over dinner. What do you say?"

"One last thing. I stated in my letter to you that I believed the stalker may be a former girlfriend."

Meadows shook his head and raised his eyebrows. "Wow, some friendships can sure end on a sour note. What happened? You have a fight over some guy or something?"

Kay leaned forward, hands resting demurely on the detective's desk. "The woman I'm referring to lived with me and was my lover for five years."

Meadows blinked twice. His face reddened. The

typing in the background stopped. The voice talking on the phone was silent. "You mean . . ." Bob said, eyeing Kay from head to toe.

"I'm a lesbian, Detective Meadows, if that's the word you're looking for."

"Yeah, right. Okay. Well, we'll look into everything." The detective stood, then bent over to pick up some papers previously knocked to the floor. "Got a pretty busy case load right now," he muttered, halfway underneath his desk. "But I'll call you if I've got any questions."

"No dinner, Detective?"

The head popped up from behind the desk. "Dinner? Oh, well, as you can see, I've got a lot of paperwork here. Better put in some overtime tonight. I'll walk you out."

"Thanks, but I can manage on my own."

Grace Perry held the coffee cup with both hands and slowly took a sip, glancing up at Kay. Her gaze was like radar. "I like what you've planned so far, Kay."

Kay shuffled the papers, restacking them into an ordered pile. "Just doing my job," Kay said matter-of-factly. This was their third meeting concerning the trip and there was something stand-offish about Grace. Kay had yet to figure it out.

"Unfortunately, you may have to make some adjustments to your timetables and plans. I have some bad news."

"What's that?"

"The trip's been delayed a month. We're not going until mid-November."

"I hope you're joking."

"Not in the least."

"What's happened? Why the delay?"

"Government red tape. I really can't tell you much more than that."

"Grace, temperatures in November and December get pretty brutal up North." Kay folded the map. "Forty below and lower. That doesn't include the wind chill. I'm going to have to order additional supplies, including protective clothing."

Grace didn't flinch. "Do whatever it takes. You've got a blank check as far as I'm concerned."

Kay's nerves were on edge. "Do you have any idea what this trip's going to be like? Does Donnelly know about this delay?"

"Yes, he knows. The new timetable was approved this morning." Grace leaned back in her chair. "I'm getting the distinct impression you don't think I can handle this trip, Miss Westmore."

"Look, my job is to get you from inspection base to inspection base. Russ's job is to set up those bases for a crew of thirty people. This trip's going to be dangerous for everyone involved. Alaska is a far cry from your desk in D.C." As soon as Kay made the last statement, she regretted it.

Grace's reply came in a cool even tone. "I'm well aware of the difference, Miss Westmore. I may be a bureaucrat, but while you're traveling from pretty park to pretty park all year long — communing with nature and picking wildflowers — I'm fighting it out in the political warrooms of our nation's capitol. And if you think that's any picnic, you're greatly mistaken."

"I was only trying —"

"Let me tell you something. I've seen it all, lady. Bribery. Scandal. Infidelity. Career sabotage. Drugs. Alcohol. Government subterfuge. Discrimination. Character assassination. I could go on and on." She leaned forward. "If you think for one minute that a little snow is going to intimidate me, you're dead wrong."

Somehow Kay remained calm. "I'm only doing the job that's been asked of me, Grace. And part of that job is to prepare you for the harsh realities of this trip."

"You've fulfilled that requirement quite nicely, thank you." Grace reached for her purse. "Now that we've got everything straight, let me pay for breakfast." As she pulled some bills from her wallet, a photograph fell to the floor. Kay picked it up. It was a picture of a young girl.

"You dropped this."

"Oh, thank you. It's a picture of my daughter, Maria. She just turned eight."

Kay glanced at the picture again. "She's beautiful."

"Yes, I think so. Unfortunately, I haven't seen her in three months." Grace's eyes glassed over. She turned away quickly, trying to get the attention of the waitress. By the time the waitress left, Grace had regained her steely composure. "I'm divorced. Vince, my ex-husband, has custody of her. It's been a rough two years. I miss my daughter very much."

Kay felt a sudden pang of remorse. After three weeks of business meetings, luncheons and breakfasts, this was the first time she'd seen the human side of Grace Perry. Still, she couldn't quite picture this cold, career-oriented woman as the loving mother of a young girl.

"Well, isn't this cozy?" a familiar voice interrupted. "I see we've progressed from the very young to the more sophisticated type. How nice."

Kay instinctively cringed. Sharp and heavy, the voice cut into her with new wounds, if that was possible. She looked up at the face that had become such a painful caricature. Not the same person. It couldn't be. "Barb. Please, not now. This is a business meeting. Important business."

Barb crossed her arms. "I have business, too. With you, Kay."

"Later. We can talk later. Call me tonight," Kay pleaded.

"What's the big idea sending a detective after me? I didn't send you any letters. Have you lost your mind or what?"

Kay looked at Grace who was staring at Barb in utter fascination. Kay struggled for composure. "Call me tonight, Barbara."

"Fine, fine," the woman barked. "I'll call you. By the way, what happened to Little Mary Sunshine? Bored with her already?"

Kay put her head in her hands. For a few seconds there was silence. Peaceful silence. Finally, Kay uncovered her face, catching Grace's eyes — unwavering and unreadable. The only movement Grace had made was to pull her chair slightly away from the table. "Grace, I'm afraid I have to apologize for Barbara. She used to have manners. Now she just has audacity."

"Oh, the big words you use now, Kay. To go with your big superiority complex," Barb said, waving her hands in disgust. "I'll be calling you tonight, you better believe it. And if you send any more detectives my way, I'll sue your ass." Barb turned toward Grace. "Kay's charming at first. But it wears off."

Barb stomped away. Kay wished she could crawl away. "I'm very sorry," Kay said, trembling. "What you must be thinking."

Grace pulled her chair back to the table. Kay watched the woman's hands as they wandered through her long, dark hair. "I'm thinking," Grace said quietly, "that your friend needs help. There's a great deal of anger there, Miss Westmore. Don't ignore it."

"Believe me, I'm not."

"The two of you had a relationship?"

"It ended last year."

"Oh, it hasn't ended, Kay. Not by a long shot."

"I guess I should ask. How do you feel about being led through the Alaskan wilderness for two months by a lesbian?"

Grace rested her elbow on the table, supporting her chin in her right hand. "To be quite honest, I couldn't care less. You're the best person for this job. If you weren't, we wouldn't be sitting here right now. You know every inch of this state and I need you."

Kay started to speak but was cut off.

"Don't misunderstand me. I care about only one thing. This job. Just make sure your ex-girlfriend doesn't interfere with your work. Are we clear on that?"

"Perfectly," Kay said, stone-faced.

Grace pushed the empty coffee cup aside. "Besides, I knew all about your lifestyle months ago. A thorough investigation was conducted on every member of the team. I intend for this project to be a success, Miss Westmore."

Kay sighed. "Can you please call me Kay? I don't think we need to be so formal."

"No, we don't." Grace draped her coat over her shoulders. "Let me tell you something, Kay. Donnelly, Eagleton and Mitchell are all planning a trip to the Oval Office for an audience with the President when this investigation's finished. But I've got news for them. I plan to be there, too. And you're going to help me."

Kay suddenly felt like a fly in a spider's web. "Seems like everyone has a personal agenda."

"Maybe. But you're to concentrate on mine. You're looking at the next Secretary of the Interior."

Kay's jaw dropped.

Grace laughed. "Oh, I know. Everyone assumes it'll be Eagleton — including Eagleton. What my friend Charles doesn't know is that I've done some heavy-duty lobbying. Charles is a poor administrator. His only strength is his friendship with the Vice President. But that may not be enough."

"I take it you think this pipeline inspection will be the weight that tips the scales in your favor."

"We'll see. The early inspection was Eagleton's idea. He approved this lovely, massive expenditure. But I'm not so sure we'll find the compliance infractions he's expecting. I've checked the reports of the last five inspections. They show the pipeline to be in acceptable condition, structurally. I made sure all the right people know that I consider this excursion into the winter wilderness to be a giant waste of time and money."

"But Eagleton said there were reports of leaks. At the initial planning meeting, you seemed to agree."

"Well, I don't know where Charles gets his information. But I have my own sources."

"What if we do find compliance infractions?"

"Oh, there'll be some. But not enough to legitimize the fuss Charles is making. He's submitted all kinds of frenetic projections to the Attorney General. Oil spills, line deterioration, poor maintenance practices — you name it. Too bad he didn't do his homework. Ever since the *Exxon Valdez* incident, the oil companies have been on top of things up here. They can't afford not to be." Grace looked at her watch. "Got to get going. Important meeting in a hour." Grabbing her briefcase, she slid out of the booth. "By the way. The conversation we just had was confidential. Any problems with that, Kay?"

"Not at all."

CHAPTER FOUR

It was autumn all over again — the dwarf birch a blazing scarlet, the willow gold and spruce a contrasting deep blue-green. Kay walked through the Riley Creek campsite at Denali National Park, surveying the area for some expansions and upgrades planned for the following spring. Suddenly she heard a woman scream, "Get out of here! Get out!"

Kay followed the voice around a culvert where the last few camping sites were located. Just west of the main path she spotted a woman, wrapped only in a towel, swatting a rather substantial-sized moose with an aluminum tent pole. The young male had caught his new antlers in the tent's support lines and was covered from head to mid-back in bright blue nylon. Thrashing back and forth, the frightened animal struggled to break free. An occasional thwack could be heard as the woman, also frightened, tried to salvage tent and belongings.

"Get out, you beast. Get out!"

Kay approached the situation warily, already trying to assess a suitable solution for both human and animal. "Miss, miss. Excuse me. Let me help you."

The woman turned, red-faced, one hand holding her bath towel in place, the other hand still wielding the aluminum pole. "Thank God. This damned beast is destroying everything. Help!"

"Miss, why don't you back away? Let the animal calm down a little. He may be able to free himself if he's left alone for a few minutes."

"He's ruining everything!" she cried. "I wasn't trying to hurt him. Just get him to leave."

Kay reached for the woman's arm. "Let's step back into the woods and see what happens. He can't do much more damage than he's already done."

Reluctantly, she followed Kay into the trees. Every so often she cursed as her bare feet came into contact with pine cones and sharp rocks.

Once into the trees Kay extended her hand to the shivering woman. "Kay Westmore, National Park Service Ranger."

"Barbara Reynolds, beginning camper."

Kay laughed along with the half-naked woman whose bare shoulders revealed a light ebony tan. The woman's red-brown hair barely reached those shoulders, framing instead the angled face and strong jaw. The two women returned their attention to the moose who had stopped thrashing and huffing and was now standing still. Occasionally, his head would move suddenly to the left or right as though confirming that he was, indeed, trapped. Then he took several steps to the right and, while walking on the tent fabric, it began to slide from his head. The moose took a few more steps to his right, continuing this movement until the nylon fabric, ropes and all, slid off like a discarded cocoon. The animal lowered his head, let out a low grunt and finally staggered forward into a fast trot through the campsite and beyond the trees until he vanished from sight.

The two women turned to each other and smiled.

"I guess I should've let nature take its course," Barb said, readjusting the towel that had slipped to reveal two sloping breasts.

"Let's see how much damage you have."

The doorbell rang and Kay jumped — from the dream and the sofa where she'd been napping.

"Instead of calling you, I thought I'd call on you," Barb said, stepping past Kay. "Hope I'm not intruding."

Kay ran her hands through her hair and tucked in her shirt. "Fell asleep on the couch. Just woke up."

Barb scanned the room like a professional cat burglar and plopped down on the overstuffed chair next to the entertainment center. "You do look a little tired, Kay. Too many late nights?"

"No. Too many fourteen-hour work days. I'm getting ready for an eight-week trip from Fairbanks to Prudhoe Bay."

"At this time of year?"

Kay watched with amusement as Barb stacked the scattered CDs that lay on top of the entertainment center into a neat and orderly pile.

"No boring office work and paper-pushing this winter." Kay sat back down on the sofa and explained what little she could about the confidential trip, trying to keep the conversation pleasant and away from touchy subject matter.

"I take it you're not traveling alone."

Kay sighed and rolled her eyes. "No."

"Your breakfast companion? Is that your traveling partner?"

"Yes. Grace Perry. She works for the government."

Barb smirked as only Barb could. "Well, I'm sure you'll manage to keep each other warm."

"Please," Kay begged. "Let's not fight."

"What's with these letters and phone calls?" Barb asked in a clipped tone.

"Someone's been harassing me. That's what."

"I would never do a thing like that, Kay. How could you even think it?"

Kay sat back down on the sofa, letting Moose, her four-year-old male cat snuggled into her lap.

Barb laughed. "That damned cat. I miss him, you know." She got up and sat next to Kay, scratching the black and white cat under his chin. "I can still picture this overgrown bag of bones sitting on the front stoop like it was his place. Remember?"

Kay looked at Barb who stared right back. Kay

could tell they were both thinking the same thing. About the day they found the cat sprawled on top of Barb's old Toyota — thawing himself on the still-warm hood. He was ratty looking and half-starved. But he was also big-boned and after a few months of a steady diet he started filling out into the incredible hulking cat. They decided to name him Moose, because of his size and how the two women had met. Tears began to flow down Kay's cheeks. "Jesus, Barb. We've got to stop this. It's too damned painful."

Barb put her hand on Kay's shoulder. "I'm sorry, Kay. Really. I am."

"I know." Kay wiped the tears from her cheeks, then looked straight into Barb's eyes. "We've got to try to be friends, Barb. All of this upheaval hurts too much."

Barb put her arms around Kay's shoulders. "Yes. It does hurt."

Kay leaned into the corner of the sofa, pulling Barb with her until they were intertwined, holding each other tightly. "Remember the day we met?" Kay asked softly.

"Yes."

"I was dreaming about it tonight before you came over."

"It all seems like a dream now. Something that happened a long time ago."

Kay chuckled. "I'll never forget the first moment I saw you. Wrapped in that towel, whacking the rump of that moose. God, what a sight."

"I must've looked pretty ridiculous."

Kay kissed the top of Barb's head. "You were beautiful. Absolutely beautiful."

"What happened to us, Kay?"

"I don't know."

"You cheated on me, Kay. I couldn't trust you anymore."

Kay sat up, pushing Barb into a sitting position next to her. Still clutching Barb's shoulders, she said firmly, "I never cheated on you, Barb. Never." Kay shook her, trying to command her absolute attention. "Listen to me. You cheated on me. But I forgave you. Each time I forgave you. But you didn't forgive yourself. So you convinced yourself that I must be cheating too. You made me a prisoner. Until I couldn't take it anymore."

"I still love you, Kay."

"Then why can't we work at being friends? Stop hurting each other."

"Friends. But not lovers."

Kay let go of Barb's shoulders. She clenched her hands nervously into fists. Biting her lower lip, she said, "That part of our life's over. I'm dating other people now."

Barb leaned back suddenly, as if staggered by a blow.

"In fact, Stef and I are dating. There's no commitment or anything, but I'm very fond of her. That much I can tell you."

Barb let out a you've-got-to-be-kidding laugh. "That child? I can understand a fling, a hop in the hay. But to say you're dating. That's downright insulting."

"To who?"

"To me. To you. Sex is one thing. Chemistry. A few hormones askew." Barb got up and began walking in circles. "But when the fire's out — you're not going to have anything left. Commitment? That young thing's nothing more than a flirt. She's using an old dyke to get some experience before she moves on."

"Maybe."

Barb grabbed Kay's shirt collar. "You're making an ass of yourself, Kay. This is just like you. Always with your head in the clouds. Miss Rocky Mountain high as a kite. You fuck a teenager a few times and suddenly you're dancing through the daisy fields of life."

Kay jerked herself away from Barb's grasp. "That's enough. As usual, things have gotten ugly. Time for you to leave." Kay shoved her way past Barb and opened the door.

"Fine, I'm leaving." Barb approached the door and, leaning into Kay's face, said, "I hope you don't get any more letters or phone calls, Kay. But at the rate you're making friends — and losing them — it wouldn't surprise me."

CHAPTER FIVE

The antiseptic smell made Kay nauseous as she walked the long hallway to her father's room. It was a weekly Saturday ritual that always seemed more like a dream than reality. Her mother had died three years ago, the victim of a stroke. That had left her father, a long-time sufferer of Parkinson's Disease, without the round-the-clock care he needed. Year after year, the crippling neurological disorder that deteriorated muscle function had slowly and painfully left her father confined to a wheelchair.

As she entered her father's room, Kay found him sitting in front of the lone window, his back toward her. He sat, his body shaking in spasms, staring at an outside world he no longer knew.

"Pop, what's up?" Kay heard a mumble or two; her father's words were often unintelligible. She approached the window and rested her hand lightly on her father's shoulder. "Hey, Pop. How you feeling?"

Kay's father raised his head slightly. "Okay," he stammered. "Cold out?"

"Actually, it's warm and comfortable in the sun, Pop. Want to take a ride outside?"

Her father's back straightened. He raised his head until his brown eyes met hers. "Out? Really?" There was a childlike light in his eyes that nailed Kay in the gut.

"Really. I'll sneak you out the back. But we'll have to put your coat on. Then we'll throw a blanket over you to keep the nurses at bay."

"Nurses. Hmmmph," her father mumbled. "Damned pains in the butt."

Kay helped her father with his coat. This took about ten minutes of struggling, pulling and tugging. With a blanket draped over his shoulders, Kay headed out the door and down the hallway. They passed the nurses' station on the left where the long corridor divided.

"Hello, Miss Westmore," one of the nurses called out. "Nice to see you."

Kay smiled. Her father grumbled another unkind epithet. "Be nice now, Pop," Kay whispered. "We're almost in the clear." Her father raised his arm stiffly and waved. He even managed a slight smile, which made Kay chuckle. "That's it, Pop. Freedom awaits us."

It took about fifteen minutes to load her father and wheelchair into the Passport. Since it was almost noon, Kay headed downtown to a luncheonette she knew her father loved.

The small restaurant had the greasy smell of plain good food not served at your local old-age home. Kay watched her father devour his lunch, barely uttering a syllable. The disease made it difficult for him to eat. Kay helped by cutting his ham into tiny pieces. But, because her father's arms constantly shook, food flew onto the floor and across the table. Kay noticed people staring but tried to ignore their rudeness. Her father was having as much fun as possible for someone in his condition. After consuming a slice of baked ham, mashed potatoes, glazed carrots, a roll and some fruit, he was ready for dessert.

"Pop, don't they feed you in that place?" Kay asked as he dug into a dish of vanilla ice cream.

"Food's terrible. No taste."

"Well, I guess we'll have to do this more often."

Her father stopped eating, a dribble of vanilla ice cream slowly finding a path down his chin. "Can we?" he asked.

Kay reached out with her napkin, gently dabbing her father's face. "You bet. As soon as I get back from my trip."

"Trip?"

"I'm going away for a couple of months, Pop. I

won't see you until after the holidays — but we can have our own celebration when I get back."

"Where?"

"A trip along the pipeline. Research work."

Her father's shoulders slumped. He continued eating his ice cream, but Kay could see the tears welling in his eyes. "Miss you." His face suddenly contorted, eyes wide with pain. "Miss your mother. You're just like her." His head fell to his chest.

Kay grasped her father's arm, squeezing it gently through the soft plaid cloth. "I know, Pop. I miss Mom too."

Back at the home the vultures circled. The head floor nurse, hands on her hips, greeted Kay and her father just inside the door. All the way to her father's room the nurse railed while Kay's temper seethed.

"How many times do I have to explain the rules to you, Miss Westmore? You cannot remove your father from the premises without advance permission." The woman was slight in stature but no less formidable. "This isn't the first time and it cannot continue."

"I had his permission and that's all I need," Kay said, continuing past the indignant woman. "Besides, I passed right by the nurses' station and no one said a thing."

"I'm well aware of that, Miss Westmore. And I've taken care of that little problem. The point is, we have rules that have to be followed. You must request permission in writing to remove your father from the premises. You're not his legal guardian."

Kay cringed. Her younger sister, Julia, was her father's legal guardian. Since Julia viewed Kay as a radical feminist lesbian ne'er-do-well forest ranger, she'd convinced the courts that she should be her father's legal guardian. It worked. Julia had taken over her father's affairs — along with any money he had left. That's why he'd ended up in this pit. With no money and no rights.

"My father's quite capable of deciding if he wants to go out or not! I asked him if he wanted to, and he said yes. I can hardly blame him."

The nurse continued to follow Kay step-for-step. "I'm going to have to speak to your sister about this. Your visiting privileges can be revoked, you know."

Kay spun around. Now she was fuming. "The hell they can! I'm his daughter. I visit him every week, which is more than I can say for his legal guardian! Would you please leave us in peace?"

"Take me to my room, Kay. This might as well be Alcatraz." Her father's voice was surprisingly strong and clear. "You leave my daughter alone. She will come and visit whenever she likes."

Kay couldn't help but smile as the nurse stomped off. Her father continued mumbling under his breath, his head swinging from side to side in anger. Once Kay arrived at her father's room, they were greeted by another sullen face. Julia. She was sitting on a chair, checking her make-up in the small mirror of a compact. She was five years younger than Kay; her bleached-blond hair and blue eyes, perfect complexion and teeth reminded her of a Baywatch Barbie doll. She had a plastic personality to match.

"Well, where'd you take Pop this time, Kay? Every time you visit there's trouble. Or so I hear."

"I took Pop out for lunch. He hates the food here, don't you, Pop?"

"Stinks," the frail man replied succinctly.

Julia ignored both her father and Kay. She removed her father's coat, helped him into his chair and turned on the television for him. "Pop, you watch TV for a while. Kay and I are going to talk. We'll be back." Julia kissed him on the cheek. He ignored the sentiment and reached for the remote.

"There's no need for anyone to get so bent out of shape. I took Pop to lunch. Big deal."

After getting two cups of coffee from a vending machine, they'd chosen a table in the nearby solarium. Julia continued her diatribe, taking over where Nurse Rachet left off.

"They're not going to let you visit anymore, Kay. You can't keep smuggling Pop out the back door without permission." Julia frowned her disapproval. Absentmindedly, she played with her hair, twirling it continuously with her right forefinger. "Suppose someone kidnapped him for real. How would they know it wasn't you?"

"No one's going to kidnap an old man with Parkinson's Disease from a nursing home. For Christ's sake, Julia."

"I'm just looking out for his welfare. I'm his guardian, don't forget."

Kay could hardly forget. Julia constantly reminded her. "Well, wouldn't it be nice if Pop's guardian visited him more often? I haven't seen you here in weeks. Another skiing trip with Jack?"

"No. I've simply been busy."

"Spending what's left of Pop's money. That's why he's in this dump."

Julia threw her head back defiantly. "Pop's money is right where it belongs. In the bank in my name. This place would've sucked him dry. I still have bills, you know. Someone has to buy him clothes, take him to the dentist, buy him personal items. But you wouldn't know about that."

Kay rolled her eyes. Last year, Kay had bought her father the first decent winter coat he'd had in years. She'd also replaced his shaver and bought him a new robe and pajamas. She couldn't remember Julia buying him a pack of gum, much less anything else. Kay guessed there wasn't much left of his money. Not after Julia and Jack's trip to Europe, the purchase of a new car and extensive remodeling of their home.

"Julia, if you weren't my sister, I'd deck you."

Julia laughed. "Kay, must you talk like that? It sounds just like something a . . . well, something a dyke would say."

"It always comes down to that with you, doesn't it?"

"Kay, you're not still upset about the court thing are you?"

Upset was an understatement. During her father's competency hearing it was Kay who had ended up on trial. Kay had no doubt it was Jack's idea. Her brother-in-law was a manipulative, scheming son-of-a-bitch who saw money at arm's reach and had happily led Kay to the proverbial slaughter at the hands of a slick local lawyer they'd put on retainer for that very purpose. Kay's lesbianism was dragged through court so that when all was said and done, her father's future was left in the hands of Julia and Jack — the perfect example of family and social integrity in the eyes of the law. But not in the eyes of her father. He had sobbed through the entire proceeding, his head bowed, eyes filled with helplessness. The last thing her father said to her that day was, "Kay, I'm so sorry. I didn't want them to hurt you."

Kay got up. She still found it difficult to be in the same room with Julia. "I've got to get going. I'll just say good-bye to Pop."

Julia smiled cheerfully. "I'll tell Jack you said hello."

"Don't bother."

As the weeks passed, Kay tried to cope with the stress of the upcoming trip, Grace's constant demands, the problems with Barb and the uncertainties surrounding her new relationship with Stef. As she stood at the bottom of the slope, she felt mentally and physically exhausted.

"Kay, look out!"

Kay glanced toward the top of the hill. Skiing down the incline and heading straight for her was Stef who still hadn't learned the art of steering.

"Shift your weight left!" Kay yelled. Too late. Kay put her arms out and caught Stef around the waist. Stef's momentum took Kay on a backward slide into the snow bank at the end of the trail. Stef ended up on top of Kay, shaking with laughter.

"I'm sorry, Kay. I told you I was a lousy skier."

Kay brushed snow from her face. "Yes, you did."

"You know, if I could learn how to steer and stop, I'd have this sport nailed."

Kay laid her head down on the snow. She was trying to control a feeling of annoyance she couldn't quite explain. Lately, she'd been short with Stef. Had cut down on the amount of time they spent together. "Hey, two minor points, believe me. I think we can start calling you Peekaboo Street right now."

"Really?"

Kay laughed sarcastically. "Sweetie, you can ski into me any time. Until I'm too old to get the hell up."

"Can I?" Stef licked some stray snow from Kay's chin.

"Yeah. Then I'll watch from the lodge in my fucking wheelchair."

"Oh, Kay. It's never going to be like that."

"No? Then why can't I get up now, damn it?"

Stef wasn't having any of Kay's bad mood, if she noticed it at all.

" 'Cause I'm laying on top of you. And that usually makes you pretty helpless, I've noticed."

"Does it?"

"Uh huh."

Stef flashed a coy little smile that drilled Kay's heart. Damn. Kay wanted to kiss her, make love to her right then and there in that snow bank. Slowly. Gently. Forever. But disaster crowded her heart. Things with Barb had failed so miserably. Stef didn't deserve a similar fate. So much of her break-up with Barb had been her own fault, Kay thought. And that thought alone was enough to make her get up. "Ready for a break?"

"Guess so."

"C'mon. We'll get something hot to drink."

Inside the lodge, Kay and Stef sat in the lounge drinking hot cider and watching the good skiers ski just outside the large picture window. Kay was in a funk and felt guilty for exposing Stef to her troubled mood. The pressure of the upcoming trip was beginning to build — and so were Kay's feelings for Stef. Something she didn't want. She wasn't ready, she kept telling herself, for this kind of gut-wrenching intimacy. She would only complicate this young woman's life and end up making her unhappy.

Kay put her mug down. "I'm sorry. I'm not having a very good day and I'm ruining it for you."

Stef put her arm through Kay's. "You've been different these past few weeks. Are you tired of me already?"

"No. It's not you at all. It's me."

"What's wrong?"

Kay struggled for the right words. "I carry a lot of baggage, Stef. A disastrous relationship with Barb that still won't go away. A screwed-up family, including a sister who loathes me and a brother-in-law who'd be happy if I were locked-up in some kind of psychiatric ward. And a job that's somehow been sucked into a political merry-go-round." Kay shook her head in disgust. "Welcome to my life."

Stef closed her eyes and took a deep breath. "Kay, I may be young and not very experienced in relationships. The kinds of problems people have and all. Why things go wrong. I only know how I felt that first day — when I saw you down by the river." She bit her lower lip, which had started to tremble. "I never wanted that day to end."

Kay put her head into her hands. "I can't. I just can't right now. I'm sorry. Maybe while I'm away we can figure this thing out."

"I understand. Really. I'm the one who pushed you. Like you said, we'll figure it out."

On Monday morning, the roar of the snowmobile filled Kay's ears as she full-throttled up the hill and began to descend the southern slope. The sleek black machine leaned her forward until she could see the flat basin of the valley spreading into the city miles below. Unlike the mountainside, blanketed in white, the city was still green — an oasis in the fall desert. The slope began to flatten into a depression cut like a shelf along the mountain. Kay downshifted until she glided smoothly to a stop near the group of watchful colleagues.

Russell smiled, approaching the vehicle with his usual carefree strut. "You've been practicing, Kay. No fair."

"Well, you never know what mode of transportation might come in handy." Kay removed her helmet. "I guess it's time to give Ms. Perry a lesson."

Russell glanced toward the shivering figure of Grace Perry, standing outside the circle of other team members who waited patiently for their turn to drive one of the snowmobiles provided for the training session. From the corner of her eye, Grace stared at Kay and Russell glumly, clearly miserable in the wind and cold.

"I'm a little worried, Kay. First of all, if she thinks it's cold now, what's gonna happen when it's forty below? And, from what she told me, she's never even set her ass on a snowmobile. I think limos are more her style."

"Probably. But she's going to set her butt on one right now. It ought to be real interesting." Kay got up, letting the machine warm-idle for its next trip. "I'll start by giving her a ride so she can get the feel of the machine. Then you can give her some simple operational instructions and we'll let her take a short ride along the flats by herself."

Russell raised his eyebrows. "Oh, boy. They just don't pay me enough for this."

Five minutes later, after helping Grace adjust her helmet and goggles, Kay took her seat on the snowmobile. "Hop on," she said, thumb pointing toward the seat behind her.

Once seated, Grace tapped Kay on the shoulder. "What do I hold onto?"

This question amused Kay. She flipped up her helmet shield and turned. With a smile she knew was more of a smirk, Kay instructed, "Put your arms around my waist. And I suggest you hold on tight."

Grace shifted uncomfortably from side to side. "Isn't there a seat belt or something?"

"No." Kay smiled again, flipped her shield back down and turned front. "Ready?" She waited a few seconds. Finally, she felt Grace's arms lightly wrap themselves around her. "Here we go."

Kay let out the clutch and throttled hard. The machine lunged forward, careening across the open flat. Grace was hanging on for dear life now, her arms a vise around Kay's waist. Inwardly, Kay laughed, knowing how upset Grace must be. The control freak — holding onto someone else for safety.

"I can't see a thing through this shield," Grace yelled to the back of Kay's neck. "How can you drive like this?"

"Sit back a little. Relax. You'll get used to it."

"You're going too fast."

"What?"

"I said, you're going too fucking fast, Miss Westmore!"

Kay smirked at Grace's obvious displeasure. It was a satisfying sound. "No need to panic, Grace. I'll slow down. Don't want you to be frightened."

"I'm not frightened! And I'm not panicking. Stop this thing!"

"Stop?"

"Now!"

Kay brought the snowmobile to a gradual halt. Before she could blink, Grace was off the machine and standing in front of her, the helmet tossed to the ground.

"Get off that thing!"

"Grace, for God's sake. Take it easy."

"I said get off that thing! I can drive it myself."

"I don't want you to get hurt."

Grace looked around. She saw Russell and the rest of the group standing at the bottom of the ridge, well out of earshot. "You listen to me, Miss Westmore. I know what's going on here. You think because you can operate a snowmobile, you're in charge. Well, you're not."

"You've already made that very clear. I'm just doing my job — which is to get us ready for this trip next week. That includes some equipment instruction."

"So, you're the equipment expert. Is that right?"

"Yes, that's right. Isn't that why you picked me for this job? And Russ? Because we're survival experts. Because we know the land."

"Get out of my way, Westmore. Now!" Grace motioned toward Kay and the snowmobile with her outstretched arm. "Move aside."

"Fine. It's all yours."

Kay took a few steps backward and watched Grace jerk the machine up the slope. She tried to banish the fervent wish for Grace Perry to smash the damned machine flush into the side of the mountain.

A few minutes later, Kay broke into a sweat just before she broke into a run. After a successful ride up the slope, Grace had misjudged the sharp incline on the way back down to the flats. The vehicle had overturned and rolled — spinning to a stop about twenty yards from where Kay began her run. Perry flopped like a rag doll, feet first down the cliffside, coming to a rest about halfway down the slope.

As Kay approached, Grace was motionless. Her

eyes were closed. Kay knelt down and put her head on Grace's chest, listening for a breath, a heartbeat. She heard both.

"I'm alive."

Kay pulled back. She noticed a slight smile on the face of the snow-covered woman.

"I believe, Kay, you may have been wishing I were dead."

"No. I was truly worried."

"Yes. It certainly wouldn't do your career any good to kill a high-level government official before we even make it into the wilderness."

Kay held out her hand. "You okay? Can you get up?"

Grace stared at Kay's hand. Then slowly, she extended her own. "I can, if you'll help me."

Kay took the gloved hand and grasped it firmly. "That's what —"

"I know, I know," Grace said, struggling to get up. "That's what you're here for. To help me."

"Just let me do my job, Grace. Okay?"

Grace wiped the snow from her jeans and coat. "Don't worry. You'll get a chance to do your job." Turning, Grace glanced toward Russell and the other team members. "You all will. I'm sure you're all feeling quite cocky right now after my little accident. But once the trip gets started, I'll be on your butts every step of the way. And if anything goes wrong, I'll kick your butts back to Fairbanks or Washington — whichever hole it was you crawled out of." Grace turned her back on the entire group and started down the hill. "This training session's over. Have a nice day."

CHAPTER SIX

Alex Chambers worked in the kitchen like a professional chef. Kay watched her slice vegetables for a salad like the Ronco salespeople she'd seen on TV. Between the slicing, sautéing and broiling, Kay was dizzy — and very hungry. As she marveled at Alex's culinary talents, she could hear Pat in the living room entertaining Stef with stories about Noah's Rainbow Inn, the Fairbanks Hotel she managed.

Alex turned the king salmon she was broiling. Then, flipping her auburn hair over her shoulder, she turned to face Kay who had begun to set the table.

"So, how're things going with you and Stef?"

"Between the trip and Barb, I can't give Stef the attention she deserves, Al. And right now, there's not much time to sort through my feelings."

"Forks on the left, Kay."

"Left?" Kay stared helplessly at the table. "I knew there was something wrong," she mumbled while rearranging the silverware.

"I know how unhappy you've been, but it seems like Stef has brought some spark back into your life."

Kay frowned. "She has."

Alex walked over to Kay and took her hands. "Then why aren't you happy?"

"Because I'm . . . afraid."

"Afraid of what?

"That it'll be a mess."

Alex tightened her grip on Kay's hands. "When are you going to stop blaming yourself, Kay? Barbara's been paving her own path of destruction for years now. Stef's not Barbara — not by a long shot."

"I don't want Stef to get hurt."

"Who says she's going to? She loves you, Kay. Any fool can see that."

"Barb loved me."

"So long as she was in control. So long as she called the shots. And that reminds me, what about these phone calls and letters? Have you heard anything from that detective you talked to?"

"He's called a couple of times. He interviewed Barb and she denied everything. Says he's still working on the case and to call him if anything else happens. I called him today."

Alex stiffened, as if to brace herself. "Why?"

"When I left work today, all the lights on my Passport had been smashed."

"Oh no, Kay. What did he say?"

"Same thing he said before. That he'd look into it."

After dinner, the music in the living room blared a South American beat. Pat was teaching Stef the finer points of the tango, marching her across the room with a plastic rose clasped between her teeth. Kay and Alex were practically rolling on the floor.

"Dum, dum, dum, da dum, da dum, da dum. Now turn," Pat instructed.

The two women made their way back to the other side of the room. Then Pat, with practiced flair, flung Stef over her arm. Unfortunately, Stef was unprepared and lost her balance, landing on the floor face down on the carpet.

"Pat, please don't throw our guests on the floor," Alex pleaded. "We have a hard enough time making friends."

"You all right?" Pat asked, turning down the music.

Stef sat next to Kay on the nearby sofa. "Fine, except for the carpet burns on my face."

Everyone laughed. Pat sat on the floor in front of Alex's chair, resting her head on her lover's knees. "We had this crazy band at the hotel the other night. Everybody ended up doing the tango. Guess that's how it got stuck in my head."

"Pat has a lot of strange things stuck in her head," Alex agreed. "Never a dull moment around here."

Leaning back, Pat waited for a kiss and got one. Then she turned to Kay and Stef. "So, what've you two been up to?"

Alex looked at Pat as though she'd just lost her mind. "Are you crazy? What the hell do you think they've been doing? Fishing down at the river?"

Pat shook her head. "You're right, Alex. Ask a stupid question . . ."

"Kay's going away soon. For eight weeks." Stef shrugged helplessly. "She's abandoning me already."

Kay ran her fingers through her hair. "Only the government would want to take a trip up North at this time of year. The assignment's not welcome as far as I'm concerned. But I've got no choice."

"What's this trip all about, Kay?" Alex asked.

"Can't really say. Just want to go and get it over with."

Stef leaned into Kay, taking her hand. "I want it to be over with too."

Alex squeezed Pat's thighs. "Oh, to be in that 'getting to know you' stage again."

Pat turned and smiled. "Squeeze my thigh again, hon — and we will be."

The conference room table was strewn with charts, maps, schedules and other assorted information. Kay had a headache. And to make matters worse, Grace Perry was hovering over her like a third grade teacher.

"Have you found it yet, Kay?"

"No." Kay waded through the stack of papers directly in front of her. "Here it is." She felt Grace's hand on her back and wondered what kind of perfume she was wearing. Something expensive. Shalimar? "The refurbishment of the buildings at Chandalar is going to cost about twenty thousand dollars, roughly."

"And Happy Valley camp?"

"Not as much. The buildings are still in fairly good shape there. Just have to set something up for food service and sewage. We're talking maybe five grand."

"Good. More money. A bigger bill for my friend, Mr. Eagleton."

"And for the American taxpayers."

Grace waved her hand in dismissal. "Oh, Kay. This comes out of an already established agency budget. I agree, it could be put to better use. And that'll be my whole campaign, from an administrative viewpoint."

"When you're the new Secretary of the Interior."

"Exactly. How quickly you catch on."

"Yeah. If I were any quicker, I'd have moved to another state by now."

Grace had a good belly laugh over that one. "You're not looking forward to our trip, are you Kay?"

Kay put the budget estimates back in the file. "What ever gave you that idea?"

"The 'I'd rather be dead' look you have on your face most of the time."

"Maybe I'm just overworked."

"Well, it's too bad. Because you have a beautiful smile."

Kay glanced at Grace over the map she was scrutinizing. "Excuse me, but was that something close to a compliment?"

"Yes, it was."

"My, but aren't we in a good mood today. What happened? Did you get invited to the President's holiday ball, or something?"

Grace returned to Kay's side of the table. She leaned against the table's edge, her thigh almost touching Kay's forearm. She was wearing an appropriately bureaucratic navy suit and sheer stockings that revealed smooth legs from knee to navy pump. "You know, Kay. If I weren't the boss, and you weren't the employee, I think we'd actually be friends."

Kay tried not to stare at those legs. "What makes you say that?"

"Because we both have a good sense of humor and we've had some interesting conversations these last few weeks. Don't you think?"

"It hadn't really occurred to me."

"We're both smart — and we know how to get things done."

Another compliment. Kay was getting spooked. "Whatever you say, Grace."

"I saw you the other night. At the university. I was just coming out of the library. You were walking down the sidewalk with a very young lady."

Kay winced. She was definitely going to stop

playing the lottery. She didn't have any luck, so why bother? "Was I?"

Grace grinned. "Yes. Anybody important?"

Sliding the manila folder into the to-be-filed pile, Kay opened the next one. "Maybe. Why do you ask?"

"Because I thought you made a lovely couple. Someone new?"

Kay rested her chin in her hand, glancing Grace's way. "Are you going to have her investigated?"

Grace frowned. "Kay, please. I'm trying to be friendly here."

Kay slapped another file down. "Are we working here, or what?"

Grace's mood did an immediate about-face. She pulled her hand from Kay's shoulder and hopped off the table. "I'll decide when we work, Miss Westmore."

"There we are. Everything's back to normal. I'm 'Miss Westmore' and you're the boss again. Just the way I like it." Kay made some notations on one of the maps.

"I'm going to get a soda. Want anything?"

"No, thanks."

Grace left the room and Kay rested her head on the table. She felt like she'd just been on a seesaw ride. And she'd been left hanging up in the air with nowhere to go but straight down.

"Miss Westmore? Detective Meadows calling. There's been an interesting development in your case. Can you come down to the station right away?"

Kay had gotten the call fifteen minutes ago. As

she drove downtown, a thousand thoughts flew through her mind of what kind of information the detective had. Did they know who'd written the anonymous letters? The person who called and hung up at least three times a day? The person who smashed her car lights? Kay was more than tired of the abuse and was ready for the answers, however disturbing they might be.

A uniformed officer escorted Kay down the same long and winding corridors she remembered from her last trip to the station. As she turned the final corner and entered Meadows' office, she was startled, though not entirely surprised, to see Barbara Reynolds seated in the chair to the left of the detective's desk.

Hearing them enter, Barb turned — eyes immediately burning into Kay's. "Kay! Thank God you're here. Maybe you can knock some sense into these people." She started to stand but the attempt was stopped by Detective Meadows, who reached out and grabbed her arm.

"I suggest you keep your seat, Miss Reynolds. Miss Westmore, why don't you sit down over here?" Meadows indicated the chair to the right of his desk. "Then we can all have a friendly little chat."

Kay sat down. How could she and Barb have been so wrong for each other? She wondered how, after five long years, they could have reached this heart-wrenching low-point? Did all love come to crash and burn? Kay could feel the heat.

"Miss Westmore, we have evidence that it was Miss Reynolds who damaged your vehicle two weeks ago." Meadows shot Barb a warning glance when she opened her mouth to speak. "We found a piece of your taillight in the driveway of Miss Reynold's home. Apparently, it got caught in her clothing and was transferred from her car to her driveway. We also found a rather nasty-looking baton in her trunk, which we believe was used to damage your car. There are matching paint fragments on the baton."

"Look, I told you I did it," Barb said with a sneer. "I admit to beating the hell out of her car. I was damned angry that night." She turned to Kay. "But, the point is, Kay — I have not been writing letters or making harassing phone calls!"

Kay rolled her eyes. "And you expect me to believe you? That's a bit much to ask, isn't it?"

"Ladies, this isn't going to do us any good," Meadows said, biting on his pencil. "The question, Miss Westmore, is whether or not you would like to file charges at this time."

"Listen, you lunkhead!" Barb leaned forward, her face hard. "Don't you get it? Yes, I nailed her fucking car — but good. But if I didn't make the phone calls and I didn't send the letters, then she's still in a lot of danger because there's some nut out there bothering her!" Barb swiveled toward Kay. "I didn't know about any of this other stuff until he told me. They showed me the letters. They're sick, to say the least. I didn't write them."

"Miss Westmore, this is the woman who's been harassing you." Meadows pointed at Barb. "We know this. The question is, what do you want to do about it?"

Kay cast her eyes toward the floor. What did she want to do? What could she do? What would her heart let her do? Somewhere beneath the hurt and frustration there was still a mixture of guilt, regret and love. She closed her eyes, wishing these moments away. But she was pressed for an answer. "I want Barb to pay for the damage she did to my car." Kay looked up at Meadows. He did not look happy.

"That's it?" he asked.

"That's it," Kay replied.

"May I make an additional suggestion?" he snapped, pushing his chair against the wall behind him.

Kay sighed, massaging her forehead. "What?"

"A restraining order."

"That's very insulting," Barb yelled, pounding her fist on his desk. "I'm not some common criminal. I'll be happy to pay for the damage I did to Kay's car. I agree, it was a stupid thing to do. But you don't have to get a restraining order. If Kay wants me to stay away from her, all she has to do is ask."

"I recommend the restraining order," Meadows stated again. "Until Miss Reynolds can learn to control her temper where you're concerned, it's the smart way to handle things."

"Fine," Kay answered weakly. "Is that all?"

Meadows nodded. "You can go, Miss Westmore." He turned toward Barb. "You stay put. We still need to talk."

Kay left the building in a daze. She stopped suddenly and looked over her shoulder. All she saw was the past — finally put to rest. Or was it?

Kay tossed and turned. She knew she was dreaming, but couldn't wake up. Suddenly, the dinner replayed in her mind like a movie reel — flickering and flashing shadows from the past. Christmas, two years ago. Was that the first sign of trouble? When the tight ball of her life with Barb had begun to unravel into anger and distrust?

Barb had invited a small group of friends for dinner: Alex and Pat, Jan and Susan, Brenda and Deborah. And Kay had invited two new friends, Peg and Sarah, she'd met on a trip to the Peninsula. They weren't a couple — just friends who had taken a camping trip to Kenai Fjords National Park. The park was 580,000 acres of coastal mountains that encompassed the Harding Icefield — a 300-square-mile remnant of the Ice Age. Kay had been assigned to a three-week patrol of the area, including some new campsites. The park was having trouble with bears — trouble caused by tourists feeding them. When Kay saw the two young women alone, she sensed that they were inexperienced campers and was concerned for their safety. She warned them against feeding any kind of wildlife and helped them stow their perishables in one of the elevated caches built to discourage foraging animals. Peg and Sarah asked a lot of questions about the area and were genuinely thankful for Kay's advice. When they left at the end of the week, they gave Kay their address.

Since Peg and Sarah lived just outside of Fairbanks, Kay invited them to the holiday party. At first, Barb seemed fine with the idea. Until that evening.

"This is just too much," Barb complained while setting out the wine glasses in two perfectly parallel lines. "Eight was manageable. But ten? Whatever possessed you, Kay?"

"They're trying to make new friends."

"You say they're not a couple?"

"No." Kay set the timer for the hors d'oeuvres — small pastries filled with seafood. "They just seemed anxious to meet other people."

"I'll bet."

"What's that supposed to mean?"

"Which one of them has an eye on you?" Barb folded her arms across her chest — a bad sign. "The forest ranger who saved them from the big, bad bears."

"Oh, for God's sake. Don't be ridiculous."

"Well, let's not forget, you saved me from that awful moose." Barb put her arms around Kay's waist. "Remember how impressed I was?"

Kay sighed heavily and backed away. "Yeah. What could I've been thinking?"

"Who'd they expect to meet here? We're all couples."

"What the hell difference does that make? We don't only know couples. Pat knows a lot of people. So does Deborah. You've got to start somewhere." Kay slammed the oven door. "Sometimes our community is just too damned cliquish."

Despite that, the dinner went fine, and later that evening, Kay went into the kitchen to make some after-dinner drinks. Peg, a part-time bartender, offered to help.

"Thanks. Professional advice is always welcome."

While making the drinks, Peg asked Kay about the Gates of the Arctic National Park and Preserve up North. "Sarah and I are thinking about making that our next excursion come summer."

"I'll get some maps and brochures for you. You should try camping near the Anaktuvik Pass. There's a beautiful Nunamiut Eskimo village located on the North Slope. A lot of beautiful rivers and lakes are nearby."

"Sounds wonderful."

"Plan your trip for July. The weather's best then."

"Cold?"

"Yes." Kay nodded. "Even in July."

"How's this for a Brandy Alexander?" Peg asked, handing the glass to Kay.

Kay took a sip. "You're hired for the rest of the evening."

"Let's see, I think we need two more of those, one Scotch and soda and a rum and Coke, right?"

"That's it."

As Peg finished mixing the drinks, the kitchen door opened and in walked Barb, scowling.

"I wondered where you were, Kay. Mystery solved."

"Peg's a professional bartender. She certainly makes a better drink than I do." Kay forced a smile. After more than three years, she could almost read Barb's thoughts. Kay could sense, almost sickeningly, the trouble that was about to start.

Barb strode right up to Peg and, without any pretense, said, "So, you're the one."

Peg set the last drink on the tray and picked it up. She looked at Barb and raised her eyebrows. "The one what?"

"The one who's after Kay."

Peg almost dropped the tray. Quickly, she slid it back on top of the counter. "Excuse me?"

"Well, I knew it was one of you."

Peg looked at Kay who looked at Barb. "Barb,

don't be an ass. Peg was helping me make the drinks. See? Here they are — and there are people waiting for them."

"Since when do you need help doing anything, Kay?" Barb brushed past Peg, reached for the tray, picked it up and slammed it into the sink. Glasses broke and liquid sprayed onto the countertops and floor.

Kay was flabbergasted. Peg rushed out of the room.

"That was really sick, Barb. What the hell's your problem?"

"I'm just trying to keep you from doing something stupid, Kay. Something really stupid."

Kay hurried into the living room to find Peg.

"Kay, Peg and Sarah left." Alex took Kay by the arm. "Peg was really upset. What happened in there?"

Kay shook her head in disgust. "We'll talk about it later."

The evening stumbled onward from there. Most of the guests left early. Only Alex and Pat lingered, helping Kay clean up, trying to be cheerful. Barb sat on the sofa; she hadn't said a word since the confrontation in the kitchen. But her gaze never left Kay, following Kay around the room like a surveillance camera.

In the kitchen Pat finally let loose. "What the fuck's her problem? That's what I wanna know. You better talk to her, Kay. I think she's gone psycho or something."

Alex loaded the last of the dishes into the dishwasher. "Pat, Kay's got enough problems right now. Don't you start."

"Start? I'm concerned about Kay. Aren't you?" Pat pointed toward the living room. "That's not normal behavior. Those poor kids were really a mess when they left."

Putting her hand on Pat's shoulder, Alex said, "I know. But I think this is Kay's call, don't you?"

Pat shrugged. "Kay?"

Kay sat down at the kitchen table. "It's true — things have changed in the past few months. I just don't know what triggered it. The jealousy, I mean." Kay looked up at her friends. "I don't know what I did."

"Nothing," Pat answered.

Alex sat down next to Kay. "Barbara's always been a little high strung. You two need to talk. That's clear."

"She's never been an easy person to talk to . . ."

The kitchen door burst open and they all turned.

Barb looked at Alex, then Pat. "Didn't anyone tell you two? This party's over."

The door slammed. The room stayed quiet. The only noise was a kind of empty static racing through Kay's mind.

Kay heard Stef in the kitchen putting away the breakfast dishes. She tugged at her backpack one last time, tightening the straps and looping them through the buckles. Kay's eyes stung with emotion. Leaving Stef was going to be a lot harder than she thought.

"Are you sure you've got everything?"

The quiet voice was tinged with sadness. Kay closed her eyes momentarily, then leaned the metal rack of her backpack against the sofa. When she turned, Stef was standing in the kitchen doorway, both hands clenched around a balled-up dishtowel. Kay swallowed hard. "I've triple-checked my list. It's all here."

"Kay, I . . ." The voice drifted into nothingness. Stef's eyes glistened and one tear fell, slowly trailing down her cheek.

Stepping forward, Kay took the towel and pulled Stef close. "No tears. I'll be back before you know it."

"Kay . . ."

Stef rested her head on Kay's shoulder. "I'm afraid."

"Of what?"

"Maybe, by the time you get back, you won't be interested in me anymore."

"Please don't talk like that."

"Well, I've been thinking. That maybe you've been right all along. That we're not good for each other. The age difference. All the pain and worry I've been causing you. All this trouble with Barb. Suddenly, it's all kinda overwhelming for me too."

"Then maybe this is a good time to say good-bye for a while. While I'm gone, it'll be an opportunity for us to think about what we want."

Stef shrugged. "I agree. I think I actually need some time away from you. There's a hurt inside that wasn't here before. We haven't had much fun lately."

"No, we haven't." Kay's stomach was burning, her mouth dry. Everything seemed to be falling apart and she was helpless to stop it. "I don't want to do this to you anymore. We don't have a commitment. While

I'm gone, you see other people. Go out. Have fun. We can talk when I get back."

"Fine, Kay. Just be careful. Please."

"I will."

Stef wrapped her arms around Kay's neck, lightly kissing Kay's cheek.

Kay gently pushed Stef away so she could see her tear-stained face. "Listen, Russ'll be flying back and forth for supplies. He said he'd stop by to let you know everything's okay."

"Tell him not to forget."

"He won't."

"Well, you better get going. Grace won't like it if you're late. No need to tick her off right from the start."

"No. Her attitude under normal circumstances is bad enough." Kay kissed Stef softly on the lips. And then she stepped away. Any further contact, and she'd never be able to leave. "Be good. You'll be able to study while I'm gone. No evening distractions." Kay picked up her pack. She didn't look back. She pictured Stef still standing in the kitchen doorway. More tears? She bit her lower lip to stop her own. What had she done? She threw her backpack onto the passenger's seat and slammed her fist against the roof of the car. She thought about what Alex had said the other night. That Barb had forged her own path of destruction. That Stef was not Barb. How true, Kay thought. No one was like Barb. No one. And somewhere in her heart, where she couldn't quite touch it yet, was the feeling that there was no one like Stef.

CHAPTER SEVEN

With an average four hours of available light, from about 11 a.m. to 3 p.m. each day, Kay, Grace and the rest of the team set out on their journey to Prudhoe Bay located just over 500 miles north of Fairbanks. The mid-November temperatures had already dropped below zero several times during the past week. Kay drove the lead snowmobile hard, its rudders gliding smoothly across the snow plains that paralleled both the pipeline and Dalton Highway to the east. Grace hung onto Kay's waist. She could feel the pressure of Grace's face against her back as they moved along at a good clip. They'd decided Grace would kill herself on a snowmobile before they ever made it to their first destination, so they would ride together with a small caravan of snowmobiles behind them. The core inspection team's first goal was to reach Livengood, a small town just southwest of the White Mountain range. It was only a short 50-mile trip, but because of the terrain and proximity to several pumping stations, it was the perfect location to launch the inspection teams.

Kay's face was covered with a warm ski mask and a pair of goggles. In these weather conditions, exposed flesh could freeze white and hard in as little as half a minute. Kay had taken every precaution for herself, Grace and the other members of their team. She had purchased the best helmets, clothing and equipment — because she knew that any problems would be on her own head and no one else's.

Except for the occasional moaning of the wind, sounds from the snowmobile engines drowned out the world that passed to the west and east. Kay was able to communicate with Grace and the rest of the team via a two-way radio system built into their helmets. But there had been little conversation in the past two hours — the vast landscape seeming to awe everyone.

The endless glaze of snow was mesmerizing. There was little depth perception across the level whiteness — which seemed to form its own dimension of nothingness leading from nowhere to nowhere. Beneath the snowy glaze lay the permafrost — a combination of gravel, sand, boulders, alluvial muck and the off-scourings of vanished glaciers and invisible mountain ranges ground to dust by 200 million years of wind and water. Above, a white sky dropped to meet a white horizon, adding to the landscape's featureless effect. Only the shadow of the pipeline itself, winding ever forward, helped Kay to focus — though her mind was more than content to wander into its own blackness, even as darkness fell around them.

After passing through three pipeline security checkpoints, the twinkling lights of Livengood finally appeared. Russell had made arrangements for their party to stay at a modest inn located on the northern end of the small town. They would be staying for several days as the first inspections of the pipeline, now visible about a quarter mile to the east, were conducted. Kay pulled the snowmobile into the parking lot. She removed her helmet and helped Grace down.

"All I want is a hot cup of coffee and a warm bed," Grace snapped as she walked stiffly toward the building. "Every joint in my body aches from the cold!"

Kay liked the feel of the small inn as soon as she entered. It was cozy warm inside. As she approached the front desk, she noticed a rustic bar and small coffee house through the door to her right. Although Russ had made the lodging arrangements for the trip, he was still in Fairbanks attending to some last-minute details. So, Kay checked in their group and handed out the keys. Remembering that she and Grace would be roommates for the next few days, Kay sighed heavily. What a way to start the trip.

Upstairs Kay fingered her own key, waiting patiently as Grace fumbled with hers.

"My hands are frozen solid. Damn it!" After dropping the key twice, Grace finally managed to open the door.

Kay edged past Grace into the room. It was small, but it appeared comfortable. "It's clean. It's warm."

"Something's missing."

Kay looked around again. "What?"

"The other bed."

Kay swung around toward the bed. It was a double bed — and, indeed, the only one. "Well, Grace, what do you expect? This was the only place available. Russ did his best."

"Oh, that's just fine. God, what a dump!"

"Well, I'm sorry it's not the Marriott or the Hilton, Grace. But this is Alaska. Remember?"

"I remember. All too well."

"I'm going to get a cup of coffee. I'll have a talk with the manager."

Kay headed back downstairs. In the small restaurant, she ordered a decaf and stared through smudged glass at the night stars against a clear sky. In the distance she could see the massive pipeline, a giant serpent fading into a black horizon. Tomorrow they would conduct the first inspections. She wondered what the results would be.

"Hey, you're Kay Westmore, aren't you? Russ told me to keep a look out for you."

Kay glanced up and smiled. A woman she didn't know was wearing a navy blue sweater and jeans.

She held a beer in one hand and a cigarette in the other. Her curly red hair contrasted with cool gray eyes.

"Lori. Lori Kincaid. I'm on the weld X-ray crew, better known as Team C. Mind if I join you?"

"Not at all."

Lori exhaled a cloud of smoke to match her eyes. "Guess we would've hooked up tomorrow, but when I saw you sitting here I thought, what the heck."

"Nice to meet you."

"Who're you rooming with?"

"Grace Perry."

Lori let out a low whistle. "No kidding. Don't envy you that. When Grace interviewed me for this job, I nearly reached out and strangled her."

"Well then, I'm surprised she's still alive. I almost did the same — and I'm sure we've got company."

"The only salvation's the pay. I'm making in six weeks what I'd make in six months under normal circumstances. Hard to turn that down."

"Definitely. Who are you with?"

"Interior."

"How'd you get picked?"

"Experience, I guess." Lori extinguished the cigarette in a small tin ashtray. "Believe it or not, I used to work for Exxon. Did a stint on the pipeline for two years. Then I moved over to the other side, you could say. Took a big cut in pay — but it eased my conscience."

"While you were on the line, you ever notice any noncompliance activities?"

"Honestly, no. But in the middle of my stint, the Valdez thing happened. I just couldn't swallow how Exxon handled things. So I left."

"A woman with integrity. I admire that."

"Yeah, well, I love wildlife. And Alaska. I'm glad to be back. Missed it a lot."

"So, you work in Grace's division?"

"Yeah. Lucky me. But I had to interview for the team just like everyone else."

"I've never seen this weld X-ray process."

"Stick with me tomorrow — and I'll show you."

"Deal."

By the time Kay got back to her room, she was exhausted. When she opened the door, the light was still on but Grace was out, snoring as loudly as a lumbermill buzzsaw. Kay undressed and rolled onto the stiff cot the manager had sent up. She closed her eyes but didn't sleep. The roar of the wild was finally keeping her awake.

The next day, the teams headed out early after a quick breakfast in the motel. Bleary-eyed, Kay staggered toward the pipeline. With her gloved hand, Kay reached out and touched one of its supports. In the section where she stood the pipe was elevated eight feet from the ground to facilitate caribou and moose crossings. Teflon-coated crossbeams held the pipeline aloft and were supported by 18-inch vertical uprights drilled 40 or 50 feet into the ground. The supports allowed the pipeline to slide three to four feet on either side in the event of an earthquake. Welded to the vertical supports were rubber bumpers that also protected the pipeline should the ground became unstable. The entire pipeline was an incredible feat of engineering that cost $8 billion to build.

Kay remembered reading that the pipeline, when full, held nine million barrels of oil, more than 11,000 barrels per mile moving seven or eight miles an hour. A major break in the line could result in an oil spill from 15,000 to 50,000 barrels. Kay watched as the three teams broke up to conduct their assigned tests. One team would walk the line for at least a mile in either direction looking for oil stains on the ground and visually inspecting welds. Another team would drop what they called "pigs" into the line at the valve stations. The pigs were devices with spring-mounted scraper blades or brushes attached to a cylindrical container of instruments. The pig moved with the oil through the pipe to record irregularities of shape or sound — like the hiss of a leak. They also loosened wax and debris from inside the pipeline. The final team would conduct weld X-rays. When the pipeline was constructed, it was pre-welded by automatic welding machines at Valdez and Fairbanks. Forty-foot pipe lengths were welded into eighty-foot double-joints, which were then transported to the construction sites. The weld X-ray team was the team Kay approached as they began their work. Kay immediately spotted Lori.

"Good morning."

"Hey! Morning, Kay. Here to learn the finer points of weld X-rays?"

"That's what I'd hoped. Say, where's the boss lady?"

Lori pulled the hood of her jacket over her head.

"Just missed her. Russell flew her up the line with B team to the pumping station above Prospect Camp."

"And I'm stuck here with C team. What a shame."

Lori laughed as she unraveled a very long strip of brown plastic. "Believe it or not, this is a giant piece of film. A little bigger than the kind you buy for your camera. The guys and I are going to wrap it around that welded section of pipe there and take a picture."

"What's the light source? I mean, it's still dark. How do you get an image?"

"Radiation — or heat, if you will. The film's heat sensitive. Since the temperature of the oil in the pipe is about a hundred and eighty degrees, that's our heat source. It'll project any weld defects onto the film."

"What do you look for?"

"A correct weld will look like a pale, textured band against the gray of the pipe. A bad one will show dark spots along the weld. Spots indicate a void left by gas bubbles. They get trapped inside the weld metal, causing corrosion and eventually, leaks."

Kay watched as the team wrapped the large piece of film around the pipe until it was clamped on the underside. The film had to be exposed for at least ten minutes. In the meantime, another piece of film was prepared for a second weld. About two hours and twelve X-rays later, a squelch from her walkie-talkie interrupted Kay's supply run for more film. It was Grace.

"Head to Pump Station Number Six and intercept the pig we just launched. I want that analyzed as soon as possible."

"When was it launched?" Kay asked.

"About ten minutes ago."

"Well, since the oil only travels about seven miles per hour, the casing won't get to Station Number Six for another eight hours, Grace."

"Go now. If you have to wait or stay overnight at the station, so be it. I don't want anything to happen to that instrumentation."

"Fine. I'm on my way."

With a sigh of disgust, Kay took out the detailed map she carried of the pipeline route. Pump Station Number Six was about thirty miles north of Livengood. It was going to be a long ride. Ten minutes later, she was ready to leave — a pack full of equipment strapped to the back of her snowmobile. She revved up the engine and off she sped, a snow cloud trailing behind her.

To the west, the pipeline zigzagged like a maze, its massive size dwarfed only by the surrounding White Mountains, frozen and formless in the dark. The gleam of the moon mirrored itself along the pipeline's surface like a laser beam directing Kay through the deep shadows.

On the way to the valve station, she was required to pass through two security checkpoints that were manned by Alyeska security personnel who patrolled the line. The Alyeska Pipeline Service Company was the consortium of eight oil corporations responsible for building and maintaining the pipeline. The checkpoint guards were less than personable. With a flashlight, they checked Kay's government-issued credentials and brusquely waved her through.

About two hours later, as dawn finally cast its golden hue over the morning landscape, Kay recognized the valve station — a large outbuilding plus a few storage sheds. Nearby, two enormous wheel valves were built into the line to regulate pressure and oil flow.

Parking her snowmobile near the station entrance, Kay shut off the motor and approached the nearby doorway. A light inside indicated the presence of a station attendant. No one answered. Kay knocked again. Still no answer. Kay knew how to intercept the instruments on her own but preferred the blessing of station personnel. After a few more knocks, Kay picked up her pack and headed toward the line. There was a ladder leading up to the valves. Slinging her pack over her shoulder, she negotiated the ladder until she stood on a small platform above the pipeline.

Kay sat down and rummaged through her pack until she found her tools wrapped in a plastic pouch. Several minutes later, she removed the plug adjacent to the main valve. She heard the whoosh of pressure as she raised the plug with its attached metal line. At the end was a magnetic plumb bob. Hours from now, when the pig had traveled the distance from Pump Station Number Five to where she waited, the magnetic bob would capture the steel instrumentation casing. Satisfied that all was well, Kay placed the plug back into position and went back to the station. It was 11:15 a.m. She estimated the casing would arrive just after five. It was going to be a long wait.

Again, Kay peered into the one-room building through cracked glass. No one home. She decided to let herself in from the cold. From her small tool kit she removed a screwdriver. It only took a few minutes to jimmy the lock. Grabbing her pack and a few other supplies from the snowmobile, Kay pushed the door wide open. A musty oily smell greeted her as soon as she entered.

Kay used her small portable gas stove to make a soothing cup of coffee and ate the lunch she'd packed. The wind was the only sound she could hear, its eerie whistle passing above and around the tiny gray structure.

Setting her wristwatch alarm for 4:45 p.m., she snuggled into the corner of the room, her sleeping bag pulled around her. She was tired from yesterday's trip and last night's fitful sleep. A nap would be just the thing — and it would be needed. She'd decided to go back to Livengood tonight, instrumentation in tow. She could feel herself drifting off, almost consciously traveling within herself to be with Stef. Spring. Warm sun. The rushing sound of river water.

"Kay, I'm so glad you could make it. I was afraid you'd decide not to join us." Sharon hugged Kay warmly, lingering for several kind moments, ending the hug with a kiss on the cheek. "I've missed you."

"I've missed you, too."

"Most everyone's at the river. It's such a beautiful day. Will you walk down with me?"

"Sure."

Sharon took Kay's hand as they left the house and started their stroll across green grasses, down the slope toward the sparkling water. Kay spied a large group of women in various stages of a picnic along the shoreline. They were cooking, eating, talking, dancing to music from a boom box. Kay said hello to a dozen or more friends she hadn't seen during the months of her self-imposed seclusion. There were many hugs and exclamations of "where have you been?" To some degree, she felt bush-whacked. Besides, she couldn't answer the question. She honestly didn't know.

Sharon saved Kay from further inquisition, shepherding her toward the nearest dock where several women sat, enjoying the unseasonably warm weather. "Oh, Kay, this is Stef Kramer." Sharon swung back toward the bank. "I don't think you've met."

"Hiya. Nice to meet you," the voice behind Kay said.

Kay mimicked Sharon's movements and was immediately slammed by the vision of sun-white blonde hair, eyes the color of fresh pine needles — a smile that was unmistakably happy. The smile touched Kay like nothing had in some time.

"Hungry?" Stef asked, blocking the sun with her hand.

"Yes," Kay said softly. "Yes, I am."

"Then follow me." Stef turned, her small frame connected by curves that ran smooth like the water below them. Kay walked awkwardly behind, suddenly conscious of her larger frame. Muscled from miles of walking. Running. Carrying backpacks loaded with equipment. Seeming so clumsy now. Hulking and unattractive. Well, what of it? It would hardly matter to this young woman. She was just being nice to an older, heartbroken dyke. Sharon had probably talked to her — wanting Kay to have some company during a difficult return to socializing.

"Do you live in Fairbanks?" Kay asked.

"Yes. I'm a student at the university. Live on campus. You?"

"Lived here all my life."

"What's your job?"

"I'm a ranger with the National Park Service."

Stef's eyes brightened. "How exciting!"

Stef directed Kay to the food. After they each filled their plates, they headed back down to the water.

"Let's sit near that big spruce," Stef pointed. "It's sunny and warm there."

Sitting at the water's edge in the heat of the sun, Kay mostly listened as Stef talked about herself, her family, school. She found herself basking, not only in the sun, but in this young woman's gentleness. And she laughed as Stef's easy humor soothed the festering wounds that had, for uncounted days, incapacitated her. She stared at Stef closely, wondering if she'd known her for months instead of minutes.

". . . anyway, I ended up sliding down the slope on my butt. It was the first time I'd ever been skiing." Stef slapped her thigh and laughed. "Oh my God, I've been blithering on like a little idiot. I'm sorry."

"That's okay. I'm enjoying it."

Stef took Kay's hand, squeezing it lightly. "Do you ever go out for a beer or anything?"

Kay shrugged. The sudden contact with Stef threw her off-guard. "Once in a while. Not very much lately."

"Do you have a girlfriend?"

"Not anymore."

"Maybe you'd like to have dinner some time."

"Sure. Why not?" As soon as she answered, Kay

wondered where the words had come from. Stef couldn't be any more than twenty-one or two. What kind of disaster was she setting herself up for? It was entirely too soon for this. Kay took her hand back and wrapped her arms around her knees. "But, then again, maybe not."

Stef's shoulders drooped, her eyes questioning the sudden change of heart. "Why?"

"I'm just not ready yet. For dating, I mean. It's too soon. But I'm very flattered that you asked. Thank you."

"Well, that doesn't mean you can't make new friends, does it?"

Kay thought about that question. The answer seemed obvious. "No."

"And you have dinner with friends, don't you?"

"Sure."

"Good. How 'bout this Friday?"

Kay laughed. She'd been artfully snookered. "Friday would be fine."

Stef lay on her side, the roundness of her breasts, the curve of her hips, the smooth tanned thighs sending Kay's mind on a frantic search for some kind of centeredness.

"By the way," Stef said softly. "I think you're the sexiest woman I've ever met."

Kay gripped the grass on either side of her, fingernails cutting through the grass into her palms. "Thank you. But I think I should be saying that to you."

"Then, why don't you?"

"Because if I do, I won't be able to stop myself."

Stef rolled over, ending up next to Kay, her

shoulder blade resting on top of Kay's hand. "Stop yourself from doing what?"

Kay could feel the softness of Stef's breast against her forearm. She looked down at the pristine face, high cheekbones chiseled beneath sun-pinkened skin. "From making a complete and utter fool of myself."

Kay woke up suddenly to the high-pitched beep of her watch. She blinked a few times, peering groggily into the blackness — trying to assess where she was. In the middle of nowhere. But that was nothing new.

Ten minutes later, her gear already packed, she was atop the pipeline with a flashlight. As she went about her work, she became acutely aware that she was alone. This was a first. She paused and raised her head, looking toward an invisible horizon. There was no shape to this world — only the shadow of the pipeline fading and thinning into nothingness. Loneliness was something that had never bothered her — at least not while she and Barb were together. Traveling and being alone were like heaven, a sense of freedom she rarely experienced while at home under Barb's watchful eye. But now, suddenly, there was an ache she couldn't quite explain. A kind of urgency in the back of her mind that pressed her to finish this job and go home. Home? Home to her had been Alaska — and anywhere the National Park Service sent her. What was it that pulled at her now? She should be happy to be away . . . from the problems with Barb, the uncertainty with Stef, the pain of her father's illness and her sister's haunting indifference. Still, she felt weirdly distracted.

A sudden wind whipped across the open tundra causing her to lose her balance. Kay fell about ten feet onto frozen ground. It was like hitting cement. She heard herself groan as she lay motionless, afraid to move. She stared at the sky and the stars and waited for the breath to ease back into her chest. Carefully, she moved her legs, then her arms. Her left shoulder hurt but, other than that, everything else seemed intact. She was lucky and she knew it. Distractions. They were always dangerous.

She managed to climb back up the metal ladder to the pressure valve platform. When she removed the seal and raised the plumb bob, the instrumentation case was there — its silver alloy reflecting Kay's flashlight. She collapsed its blades and pulled it through. Carefully, she packed it in a specially padded carrier with Velcro closures. A few minutes later, she was at the controls of her snowmobile heading back to Livengood.

At the hotel, she found a visitor waiting for her in the small lobby. Detective Meadows. She hardly recognized him dressed in casual clothes and a parka.

"Miss Westmore. Glad I was able to intercept you on the early part of your trip. We need to talk."

"Has something happened?"

"I'm afraid so." The detective pointed to the coffee shop. "You look like you could use a cup of something hot. We can talk more privately."

"Fine."

Meadows methodically doctored his coffee with four creams and three packs of sugar while Kay glared and waited, imagining the worst. After watching the spoon circle the cup for about the hundredth time, Kay was ready to throttle the news out of him.

"Detective?"

The spoon hit the saucer with a loud clank. "Yes? Oh, of course. Why am I here?"

"Yes. Why?"

"Miss Reynolds is on the loose again."

"On the loose?" Kay asked with uneasiness.

"She tried to set fire to your apartment building. Apparently, she didn't know you were away."

"Oh, my God." Kay fell back against the booth. She hit her injured shoulder and winced. "Was anybody hurt?"

"Fortunately, no." Meadows flipped open his small spiral notebook. "Your downstairs neighbor — a Mr. Hall, I believe . . ."

"Yes, Carl."

"Carl Hall — right. He caught Miss Reynolds in the upper hallway with a can of gasoline. She had doused a large area outside your front door and was making her way down the stairs." Meadows smirked approvingly. "This Mr. Hall tackled her. He yelled for help and the friend who was watching your apartment for you — a Miss Kramer — heard him screaming and called nine-one-one."

"I can't believe this."

"We're holding Miss Reynolds and your neighbor, Mr. Hall, is pressing charges. He's pretty pissed off, as you can imagine. She bit him a few times. He had to be treated at the hospital."

"Jesus. She's really flipped."

"To say the least. Know what she said when I finally talked to her?"

"I don't want to hear this."

"You better hear it. She said, and I quote..." Meadows flipped to the next page of his notes. " 'I wanted to burn her and that little whore she's been fucking behind my back to a satisfying crisp.' " The detective slapped the notebook down on the table. "Now, are you going to press charges?"

Kay didn't hesitate. "Yes, of course. I have to. She could've killed them and everyone else in the building."

"How long will you be away?"

"Until after the holidays."

"Okay. I'll keep in touch."

Kay rubbed her eyes and tried to ease the tension in her neck by moving her head from side to side. "What could I have possibly done to make her hate me so much?"

Meadows lowered his head, eyes finding Kay's. "Now hear this, Kay. You're a fixation. You're not the problem. She is. Trust me. I've seen this before. It's an obsession. Someone who's an over-achiever, a perfectionist, demands order and is extremely controlling. That's the profile."

Kay blinked in surprise. "That's Barb."

"Exactly. And you became a part of the little box that was her world. Without you, there's no box. No security. Without a successful job there's no box. Without complete control, there's no box."

"Suffocation."

"Excuse me?"

"Nothing. Just thinking out loud. Thank you, Detective. You've been very helpful."

"You can call me Bob. I promise I won't try to hit on you again."

Kay smiled. "Thanks, Bob. Please call me as soon as you know anything."

Kay opened the door to her hotel room quietly. It was after 10:30 and the room was dark. By the time she showered, changed and hit the cot it was almost 11:30. Grace seemed to be asleep, so she pulled the covers up and turned off her light.

"Did you get the casing?" the voice behind her asked matter-of-factly.

Kay bristled. Yes, she thought, and I almost killed myself, too. "The Team B technicians already have it."

"Good."

Kay turned over on her back. She let out an involuntary moan. Her shoulder was throbbing, her back sore. And her head was pounding — no thanks to Barb who, even from fifty miles away, could reach out a hand to slap her silly with fear.

Grace's light clicked on. "Are you all right?"

Kay turned her head slightly. "Nice of you to ask. Actually, no. I fell. Seem to have wrenched my shoulder."

"Fell! From where?"

"From the valve platform. It was a bit of a jolt."

"Christ! Why didn't you say something?" Grace

got up and walked over to the cot. "Let me have a look at that shoulder."

Kay glanced up at Grace. The woman was actually quite beautiful, Kay thought. Dark brown hair falling haphazardly over shoulders. Eyes like golden almonds.

"Well?"

"Really, Grace. It's okay. Just sore." Now Kay stared at Grace with suspicion instead of interest. Why should she care anyway? She'd been an absolute bitch from day one.

Grace stooped at the edge of the cot. "Let me see it." The voice was edgy.

Kay knew that tone — commanding. It reminded her of . . . someone. Reluctantly, Kay turned over, her bad shoulder elevated.

With unexpected gentleness, Grace rolled back the sleeve of Kay's T-shirt. "Can you move it?"

Kay raised her arm as far as she could. "I can move it, it's just sore."

"Well, you've got a bad bruise and the shoulder seems swollen. I'm going to call Dr. Norris. He's an excellent physician."

Despite Kay's objections, the doctor assigned to their excursion was summoned. Her shoulder was wrapped and she was given an ice pack. He had a brief conversation with Grace and left.

"You're to keep the ice pack on it tonight and tomorrow. It should start feeling better in a couple of days," Grace said, returning to bed. "If you lie on your side, I'll help you with this ice pack."

Kay stayed on her side, facing the opposite wall. Grace slipped the ice pack underneath the outer wrappings of the elastic bandage.

"Thank you, Grace. I appreciate your help and concern."

"Oh, please. Don't go getting the warm fuzzies, Miss Westmore. I can't afford to have you injured. That's the bottom line."

Click. The light went out.

Kay clenched her jaw. She should've known better. There wasn't a compassionate bone in that woman's body. "Of course," she answered with feigned indifference. "Goodnight."

The phone rang incessantly. Finally, as Kay was about to hang up, Stef answered.

"Stef, it's Kay. You all right?"

"Guess you heard about the trouble."

"The detective paid me a visit last night."

"I'm really sorry, Kay. You must be very upset."

"My main concern is you. I don't want you staying there anymore. Go back to the dorm — or stay with Alex and Pat. I know they wouldn't mind."

"I'll go back to the dorm. I'm here because I thought you'd be calling. I was just coming up the stairs when I heard the phone."

"Well, so long as you're safe, that's all I care about. If anything happened to you, I'd . . ."

"I'm all right, Kay. Thanks to Carl."

"I owe him a big fat kiss."

"I'll tell him."

"Please do."

"How're things at the pipeline?"

"Cold. Windy. Lots of snow."

"Sounds like Alaska."

"True enough." Kay hesitated. "Are you behaving yourself?"

"Depends on what you mean by behaving."

"Having fun? Studying? Going out with friends?"

"Oh. Well, in that case, no."

Grace passed by the phone and gave Kay the evil eye. The team was about to leave. "I've got to go, Stef."

There was an audible sigh. "Kay, I miss you."

"I miss you, too."

CHAPTER EIGHT

Kay sat stiffly, sipping a cup of coffee. She was exhausted. After two weeks of terrible weather and twelve-hour days running up and down the line at Grace's every command, she'd almost had it. The full team had finally reached Coldfoot the day before. The first day of December had recently dawned at a few minutes past 11:00. It was a balmy thirty degrees below zero outside.

Lori sat across from Kay lost in the same kind of exhausted stupor. They were roommates now for the next three days. The inn at Coldfoot, the only inn located in this town of 35 inhabitants, was uncomfortably chilly.

"Hope Grace doesn't find us in here goofing off. She'll have our heads," Lori said, clearly unconcerned.

"We've been at it since five o'clock. I think we're entitled to a break."

Lori blew on her fingertips. "Don't they have any heat in this place?"

"Apparently not. Everyone looks well-preserved around here."

"Ladies, ladies! Have you come inside to warm your tootsies — or to get away from Grace?"

Kay chuckled. It was Russell, his large frame made even bulkier by the parka he was wearing.

"To get away from Grace," they said in unison.

"Funny how I knew that." Russ served himself a cup of coffee. "I just got finished escorting her highness up to Dietrich Camp and back. Don't ask me why. We didn't even land."

"Aerial scouting?" Kay asked. "Not much to see from a helicopter at three thousand feet."

Russ sat and stroked his beard, which usually meant a conscious revelation was just around the corner. "No, but, you know, as grumpy as that dame can be, I've got the sneaking feeling she knows exactly what she's doing."

Lori, sitting on her hands to keep them warm, nodded in agreement. "Trust me, Grace knows exactly what she's doing. She's incredibly smart and knows how to play the political game. A lot of folks have crashed and burned around her since I've been with Interior."

"That doesn't surprise me," Kay said.

Russell looked out the window. "Well, here's the

rest of the news. Grace wants to visually inspect every inch of the line between Coldfoot and the old Gailbraith Camp. We've got a week to get it done."

"Christ, that's over a hundred miles." Kay shook her head. "That's a tall order."

"Yeah, it is." Russ got up and stamped his feet. "Tomorrow, she personally wants to go up to Wiseman then back to Dietrich Camp. I think she wants you to take her by snowmobile, Kay."

"What does she want me to do, stop every eighty feet?"

"You hit the nail on the ol' head. She told me to pack all the camera equipment. I'm supposed to fly to Wiseman and leave additional supplies at Ranger Cabin four-oh-five in Gates of the Arctic just east of North Fork River." Russ handed Kay a map. "It's all detailed here. I worked it out for you."

Lori let out one of her patented whistles. "That's gonna be some trip. The weather's supposed to be shit after tomorrow. I've been getting regular updates every few hours on the radio."

Kay started to pace. "She's going to kill us all before this is over."

"I'm not only going to stock the cabin west of Wiseman for you, Kay — but both cabins north and south of four-oh-five in case you run into any snags. Whatever you do, hang onto that map."

"Yeah, I will. Thanks, Russ."

"If the weather doesn't turn on us, I'll fly up Wednesday and wait for you at Dietrich Camp."

"I'll be there too," Lori said. "Will you take me with you, Russ?"

"Sure."

Kay opened the door and a gust of wind rushed

in. "Thanks, guys. I'm going to check on some supplies myself. Then I'm going to talk to Grace."

"Kay, wait!" Russ came out after Kay, grabbing her shoulder. "Kay, I . . ."

Kay looked at her friend's deep-set eyes. They seemed troubled. "I'll be okay, Russ. Don't worry."

"It's not that. I don't know if I should mention this, but . . ."

"But what?"

Russ almost mumbled the words. "I went back to Fairbanks for supplies. I saw Stef."

"Is she okay? Something wrong?"

"Well, no . . . she's okay. I told her you were fine. She was relieved, but . . ."

"Would you spit it out already?"

"She was with somebody else. Stef introduced her to me as a friend from school. But she looked kinda funny . . . like she was sorry I'd seen them."

Kay's mind went blank. Thoughts of Stef raced away even as her heart grabbed for them. "Hey, no problem, Russ. We didn't have any kind of commitment or anything. But thanks for telling me."

"I didn't really want to . . ."

"It's okay, Russ. Really." Kay went in search of Grace. In search of anything that would take her away from that moment.

That night, Kay went to bed early. She and Grace were leaving at five a.m. As much as she'd tried, she could not talk Grace out of the solo trip. It was dangerous for ten people, much less two. But Grace was adamant and Kay was disturbed and puzzled.

Why Wiseman? It wasn't one of their original destinations. It'd never been brought up in any of the preliminary plans. When Kay pointed this out at a meeting earlier in the day, she was immediately rebuked.

"Just do your job, Miss Westmore. And I'll do mine."

"The weather's supposed to turn, Grace. Snow has been forecast for Wednesday through Friday."

"If I stopped this operation for every weather forecast I received from your *friend*, I'd still be in Livengood."

Kay didn't like Grace's sarcasm. "Lori's just doing what you asked."

Grace sneered. "I knew you two would be pals. Wasn't hard to predict."

"What's that supposed to mean?"

"Well, you're both of the . . . persuasion, shall we say? So, I just naturally assumed . . ."

Kay threw her pen down, stopping Grace in mid-sentence. She was fuming. "Be careful what you assume, Grace. Lori and I've become friends, that's true. But it's strictly platonic, I can assure you. Not that it's any of your damned business."

"Watch your mouth, Miss Westmore. It is my business. Everything on this trip's my business. Don't you forget it."

Hours later, Kay still felt the sting of Grace's words. She tried to sleep but couldn't. Her thoughts had turned to Stef. Should she be surprised that Russ had seen her with someone else? She had practically shoved Stef in that direction, knowing all the time it wasn't what she really wanted. It had never been what she really wanted.

Their love-making had become synchronized to familiar touches, to the kind of pleasure they each wanted to receive and to give. Stef leaned over Kay and whispered, "I love you," while she explored the wetness between Kay's thighs. Kay touched Stef's cheek and smiled.

Closing her eyes, feeling Stef inside her — Kay braced herself against the heat of Stef's touch, the strength of the intimacy and its hold over her. To let go completely was what she really wanted; both her body and Stef knew how to take her there. She bore down on Stef's hand, surprised by the strength of the orgasm, coming in waves. Stef kissed her and pulled her close, the final thrusts of her hand molding Kay tight into her arms.

And then she wanted to say it. How much she loved Stef, how much their togetherness had finally smothered the hurt of the past. But the words got caught in her throat. The image of Barb was still stuck in her mind like a roadside car, ditched and going nowhere. Stef continued to love her and the words continued to stick. All Kay wanted to say was left unsaid, until another orgasm passed through her.

Kay jumped when she heard Lori come into the room. The shower went on and about twenty minutes later, Lori got into her bed.

"Hey, Lori."

Lori looked over toward Kay. "Thought you were asleep."

"No. I've been thinking about the trip. Besides, it's freezing in here."

"You can say that again. I've got my long underwear on. Not what I'm used to sleeping in."

Kay heard her get up. The overhead light flashed on. Kay watched as the woman scurried around the room to the small closet. Lori was, indeed, clad in long underwear — tightly outlining an attractive if somewhat ample figure. She was about Kay's size, but fleshy instead of muscular. Her body reminded Kay of a Rubens painting — deliciously pear-shaped.

Kay watched as Lori dug out the two camping blankets they owned plus two extras provided by the inn. Kay got up to help remake the beds using every available cover.

"There," Lori said proudly. "Maybe we'll make it till morning."

Lights out, Kay drifted off into a restless sleep. The weight of the blankets threatened suffocation and she was still cold. Some time later, Lori climbed in with her.

"I know you're not asleep."

"I've been dozing. That's about it."

"I'm not trying to get funny with you, Kay, but I need some body heat or I'm gonna die."

Kay turned over and accepted Lori into her arms. "That's okay. Grace thinks we're having a raging affair anyway."

"You're kidding?"

"Nope."

"That woman is enough to drive anyone nuts."

Lori rested her head on Kay's shoulder. "You have a girlfriend at home?"

Kay hesitated. What was the answer? "I'm not sure. How 'bout you?"

"Yeah. She's great. Stacy. We met last year at an AIDS fund-raiser in Washington. It was love at first sight. At least for me."

"That's nice. Guess Stacy wouldn't approve of this."

"I don't know. She's pretty cool. And I think she'd rather have me alive than sent back as a frozen Popsicle."

"Well, you're welcome to stay. I feel better already. For the warmth and the friendship."

"Me, too." Lori put her arm around Kay's waist. "You be careful on this trip, Kay. I'm going to be worried sick."

"I will."

"Russ and me'll be waiting at Dietrich Camp."

"Keep a spot warm for me, will you?"

"You bet."

The trip north to Wiseman was slow, hampered by stops almost every eighty feet along the line. While Kay walked beneath the elevated sections of pipeline, Grace sat like a queen in the snowmobile, taking notes and barking commands. In the darkness Kay used a flashlight to illuminate each weld, looking for any signs of leakage on the pipe itself or the ground underneath. Grace decided which welds to skip — and they didn't skip many. For the last three hours, Kay hadn't shifted the snowmobile out of second gear. As they crawled forward, Grace would suddenly say, "This one. Stop and check this one." Kay would idle the machine and get out, forced to control her anger and to keep herself from snapping, "Go check it yourself." Once under the weld, Kay would give a curt verbal report, "No visible damage." Grace would sometimes order her to document a particular weld or stretch of line by taking photographs. During the brief daylight hours, Kay used high speed film. In the darkness, she used infrared. She juggled cameras like a circus performer, her hands frozen and barely able to manipulate the equipment. All the while Grace never let up. "Stop here. Be sure to check the top of the weld. Dig into the snow to check for old oil stains. Take photographs." On and on until Kay began to think of Grace as a drill instructor rather than a colleague. Once, when responding to one of Grace's many commands, Kay replied, "Yes, sir!" Grace actually stopped writing. Kay saw the mere hint of a smile. Then, just as quickly, it was gone and the long, monotonous ordeal began again.

Grace bullied her way through each Alyeska security checkpoint as though she were the President. The guards seemed genuinely intimidated as Grace announced who they were and what their business was. Kay stayed in the background. Each time, the guards passed Kay and Grace through the gates quickly, relieved to be rid of them.

As the first day waned, Kay warned Grace that they needed to move more quickly in order to reach the pre-stocked cabin still about eight miles away. It was after ten o'clock at night and the temperature had dropped well below zero.

Grace finally relented. "All right, all right. But we're going to have to backtrack tomorrow. I don't want to miss an inch of this line."

Kay still couldn't figure out Grace's obsession with this section of pipe, but she didn't argue. Her main goal was to get them to shelter for the balance of the night. Putting the snowmobile into high gear, Kay sped farther north with Grace in tow.

The ranger cabin, located on the eastern border of the Gates of the Arctic National Park and Preserve, was freezing inside. But Kay soon discovered that not only had Russ stocked the shelter with food, gasoline, blankets and other necessities, but he had also left a kerosene heater set up and ready to operate. As its warm glow filled the one-room structure, Kay said a silent thank you to Russ for his careful planning.

For the next ten minutes, Kay unloaded the snowmobile while Grace warmed herself by the heater. Kay was beyond thinking it might occur to Grace that she could use some help. The woman was one-dimensional. She clearly thought only of herself.

When Kay finally sat down with a hot cup of coffee and a bowl of freeze-dried soup brought to life with boiling water, Grace gave her a "where's mine" look. Kay ignored her, positioning herself comfortably against the wall, her numbed legs stretched toward the heater. Finally, Grace got the message that Kay wasn't about to wait on her. Grace stomped toward the portable stove and made her own coffee.

"Not going to eat anything?" Kay asked. "There's all kinds of soup, crackers, some canned stuff you can heat up."

Grace gazed with obvious contempt at the canned goods that lined one of the built-in shelves. "Oh, yummy. SpaghettiOs. Russell's certainly a connoisseur of fine food."

"Well, I guess he forgot to order the caviar. Sorry."

Grace plopped back down next to the heater. "I know you think I'm a snob. True, I haven't eaten anything out of a can since I was fifteen. Not since those summers I spent with my father in Harrisburg. He made something out of a can every night when he wasn't drunk. When he was smashed, whatever was in the can usually ended up burnt beyond recognition at the bottom of the pan. But I still had to eat it anyway. I don't know if you've ever tried charred Chef Boyardee ravioli, but it's not very appealing — not even to a ten-year-old."

Kay was stunned by the sudden humanness. "No, I guess not. Were you born in Pennsylvania?"

"No. Cleveland. When my parents divorced I was only nine. My father moved to Harrisburg. I visited him every summer for six weeks until I was fifteen. I guess that's why I always loved school so much. Because I dreaded summer."

"Your father was an alcoholic?"

"Uh huh." Grace talked about herself as though it were a clinical summary of someone she hardly knew but had read about in a medical journal or fiction novel. "For six weeks every summer he was drunk each weekend and a couple of times during the week. When he drank, he raped me. It was a fairly consistent pattern until, as I said, I was fifteen."

Kay almost dropped her coffee mug. She didn't know how to respond. Grace didn't seem to notice or care because she kept right on talking.

"Went through the whole analyst thing. Tried to save two marriages — but the walls kept going up. The only thing I have to show for any of it is my daughter, Maria." Grace extended her hands toward the heater. "And now my husband has her."

"You have visiting rights?"

"Of course. It's the best that could be arranged for right now."

"I'm sorry."

"Why? It's not like I've treated you very well. I'm a hard person, I know. Don't have many friends. Live for work and my daughter." Grace reached out and squeezed Kay's arm. "It's been hard working with you."

"Really?"

"Yes. I like you, Kay. And quite frankly, I don't want to. With very few exceptions, the people I've ever liked or loved ended up hurting me. Trust does not come easy."

Kay shrugged. "I've got no reason to want to hurt you, Grace. I've done everything I can to make this project work for you."

"Yes, well. At least something's going right. No leaks. No bad welds. No structural problems." Grace leaned back on her hands and cocked her head to one side. "This section of the line is the one Eagleton got the bad reports on." Grace laughed. "Poor Charles. I have to brief him in a few days. He will not be a happy man."

"Guess not. You must be pleased."

"Well, my personal life may be a wreck, but my career's on the right track. I should at least be thankful for that."

"Depends on what's most important."

"It's just reality, Kay. I can deal with the hard, cold facts — and leave emotions to others."

Kay studied her closely. The woman's eyes were dull, face lined. She didn't believe a word Grace had just said. "Sounds like a lonely philosophy."

"When you're alone, what does it matter?"

The weather had turned even before Kay and Grace set out the next morning. It was a light snow that gradually intensified. Kay suggested that instead of backtracking, they follow the pipeline directly to Dietrich Camp, still about thirty miles away. Surprisingly, Grace agreed. Her demeanor had changed since last evening's revelations, all of which Kay was still digesting. Though she issued commands at an unrelenting pace, Grace seemed less abrasive. Kay wondered how long the transformation would last.

The storm worsened at an alarming rate. Kay was having trouble with visibility and road conditions. The Dalton Highway had a reputation for being rough — ruts, large rocks, soft shoulders and steep inclines. "Highway" was much too kind a term. It was a travel-at-your-own-risk proposition.

As a result of the weather, the pipeline inspection was abandoned. Their only mission now was to make it to Dietrich Camp. As the snow fell, Kay strained to see the road. Her mind drifted as the snow did. She remembered a skiing trip she'd taken with Barb, a kind of honeymoon to celebrate their first year together.

The resort was everything they'd hoped it would be. The view from the mountain had been spectacular and the conditions almost perfect. Like now, there was a continuous snowfall that draped the trees and cliff-rock until all was white and dreamlike. A lodge, with an aura of seclusion, had been built into the mountainside.

Their dinners were candlelit, their love-making passionate, their hold over each other electric. They talked and laughed and loved, aware that they were making memories.

And Kay did remember. She remembered the flicker of candlelight in her lover's eyes, the clinking glasses of champagne, the illusion that time was somehow at a standstill. Everything was perfect.

On Saturday night, over dinner, Barb had poured two more glasses of the iced champagne and said, "I do want to thank you for your patience these last few months. This Civic Center project's really taken a toll on me. But it's a big career boost."

"Your design for the center is fabulous. I'll be surprised if the firm doesn't offer you a partnership."

"They will. And then we'll really celebrate."

"What could be better than this?"

"A trip to Europe. Paris. London. Wherever we want to go."

"Oh, you know me by now. I'm a homebody. I don't need a fancy trip somewhere to enjoy you."

"That's what comes with success and power, Kay. You've got to live a little. And I plan to."

"Good. You deserve it."

Barb redeployed her silverware, lining it up in perfect symmetry with the china. "I've planned my moves upward in the company step by step. I started lobbying for this project months ago. That's the way you have to play the game. Deliberately."

"I admire your ambition. I've always been content to stay in the background."

"Not me. I can look ahead five years from now and see everything laid out in front of me like a road map."

Kay leaned back as the waiter delivered her meal. She placed the cloth napkin on her lap. "In my experience, it's not always easy to control everything that's going to happen. But I guess that's because nature's my business — and nature's unpredictable. Sometimes you have to go with the flow."

"Like the moose knocking over my tent?"

Kay chuckled, cutting into her baked potato. "Exactly! You didn't plan that to happen. Did you?"

"Hell, no. But I took control of the situation. Pretty damned fast."

"Funny. That's not how I remember it." Kay pointed to herself with her knife. "I came to your rescue, if you recall."

"Did you?" Barb's eyes twinkled in the candlelight. "How do you know I didn't lure you to that campsite with my pitiful cries for help?"

"You didn't even know I was there!"

"Kay, my darling, I had my eyes on you for days.

Love, more than anything else, requires the most thoughtful planning of all."

Kay was skeptical, to say the least, but she let it pass. "And what are your plans now — since I've been officially lured, that is?"

Barb moved the table's centerpiece aside. "Well," she whispered. "After dinner, I'm going to order another bottle of champagne. Then, we're going back to the room and I'm going to make love to you all night long."

"Sounds well thought out."

"I think so. By the time we're finished early in the morning, you'll be whispering my name forever."

Forever. That's how long it was going to take Kay and Grace to get to Dietrich Camp. The cold was biting; it penetrated every protective layer. Kay had never been this cold before. The frigid air hovered like death and for the first time she was afraid of the elements. Truly afraid.

Behind her, Grace was yelling, "Kay, we've got to keep going. Do you hear me? Keep going, or we're going to freeze to death!"

No, that wasn't right. If they kept going they'd definitely freeze to death. They had to find shelter. Kay focused on the road ahead. They were still too far from the northern ranger cabin to make it. And they certainly weren't going to make it to Dietrich Camp. Up ahead she spotted a grove of pines to the east. She swerved the snowmobile toward them. They would have to construct their own shelter or they would both die.

"Kay, what are you doing? Damn it! You keep going, do you hear me?"

Grace's face was buried in Kay's back. Kay could barely hear her through the microphone. Disoriented and weak, they were both suffering from the early stages of hypothermia.

"I'm trying to save our lives, Grace. We're in big trouble here."

"Get this damned machine back on the road, Kay. That's a fucking order!"

"Shut up, Grace. For once, just shut up!"

Kay stopped the snowmobile in the middle of the pine grove where she saw a depression in the snow. She ordered Grace to sit on a blanket near the snowmobile's engine for temporary warmth, then she went to work.

With a collapsible shovel she dug out the depression within the circle of pines, clearing away the new-fallen snow. Underneath the new snow there was a layer of ice, which she cut into blocks with a sharp knife. She used the ice blocks to reinforce the trench walls. In the depression she set up the tent; it was recessed into the ground for added protection. Over the tent she anchored a plastic tarp to serve as a double wind-block. By the time she finished, she had to carry Grace inside. She had passed out and was moaning soft, inaudible words.

Kay got the last of the supplies she needed, then shut herself inside with Grace. She lit the small portable stove that ran on white gas. It would radiate some heat. She also lit the lantern that would provide light for up to thirteen hours. It, too, would give off a tiny amount of heat.

Unrolling both sleeping bags, Kay placed one

inside the other for double insulation. She took off Grace's wet clothes, boots, socks. She replaced the damp socks with two pairs of dry ones and slid the woman, dressed only in thermal underwear, into the double sleeping bag. Ten minutes later, she made some tea. She coaxed Grace into consciousness and made her drink a few sips at a time.

"Where are we?" Grace asked weakly.

"In a hole in the ground."

Grace looked at Kay and started to laugh. "Are we dead then?"

"Not yet."

Kay crawled outside briefly to fire up her walkie-talkie, but the storm was so powerful that all she received was static. It didn't take long for her to give up and go back inside.

Taking off her own wet outer clothing, Kay also slipped on new socks. Then she melted some more snow for soup and tea. When Kay was satisfied that Grace had eaten enough, she shut off the lantern and portable stove. Their hole in the ground was pitch black.

"Shove over," Kay said, as she started to squeeze inside the sleeping bag next to Grace.

"I beg your pardon." There was the slightest hint of familiarity to the edge in Grace's voice.

"Do you mind?" Kay asked sarcastically.

"No. I'm sorry. Of course not."

"Where did you think I was going to sleep?"

"My brain cells aren't working too well right now."

Kay didn't answer. She slipped in next to Grace and pulled the top of the sleeping bag over their heads. As she lay there, she tried to figure out what to do with her hands. Funny. This had never been a problem before. Finally, she rested one hand under her head and the other on Grace's shoulder. She was shocked when, without a word, Grace pulled Kay's hand and arm around her waist. It was the last thing she remembered.

Morning came without light. Kay had grown accustomed to it now. She pushed the tiny button on her watch to illuminate its dial. It was 7:30. Grace was still asleep. Kay lay on her back staring up into the blackness, thinking about Stef. Not knowing if love had already been lost somewhere across the miles of line where she could not touch it, could not even sense it.

She remembered the last time they were together, when Stef had said, "You see someone . . . or you make love to someone — and you don't know it's the last time. Not until later." A tear had fallen and Stef wiped it away with the heel of her hand. "Then you wished you knew. Maybe you would've said something different. Or tried harder to remember those last moments."

Kay pushed the memory away and turned on the lamp. A trail of light, like an errant moonbeam, made an irregular pattern through the tent — a soft glow that turned darkness into shadow. Kay also lit the stove. With a whoosh the fuel ignited, giving off some welcome heat. The cold no longer lay as heavy in their insulated cocoon. But she could still hear the wind, thumping hard against the tarp and tent. The storm was not finished with them.

Kay slid out of the sleeping bag, started some coffee boiling and brushed her teeth with cold snow water. Breakfast looked like freeze-dried eggs and ham. The directions on the packages were always the same: "To prepare, just add boiling water."

"Are we still trapped in this arctic hole?"

Kay glanced over her shoulder. "I'm afraid so."

Grace was sitting up, rubbing her eyes with her fingertips. "Can you get us out?"

"I haven't checked the exact weather conditions yet. But probably not today."

"Damn!" Grace lay back down, hands resting beneath her head.

"Coffee?"

"Yes. Thanks."

About two hours later, they were back in the sleeping bag. There was no point getting fully dressed. The only sure way to keep the cold at bay was to stay inside the double insulated sleeping bags and share body warmth.

"I know you have family, Kay. Tell me about them."

"Huh?"

"Family. Back home?"

"Oh, yeah. My mother died three years ago. But my father's still alive. Unfortunately, he's ill, so he's in a nursing home. And I've got a younger sister."

"Do you see them much?"

"I visit my father as often as I can when I'm not traveling. Two or three times a week. I don't see my sister on a regular basis."

"Why?"

"We don't get along."

"That's too bad."

"She doesn't agree with my . . . lifestyle, shall we say."

"What about your father?"

"He doesn't care — so long as I'm happy."

"Sounds like a great guy."

A chill ran through Grace. Kay could see it visibly shake the woman. Grace buried her head in Kay's shoulder against the cold. Kay pulled Grace closer.

"No sun today, not even for a few hours." Kay rubbed Grace's shoulders.

Grace smiled weakly. "Why are you being so nice to me, Kay? You should've left me out in that hellish storm. It's what I deserve."

"Don't be ridiculous."

"You saved our lives. Thank God, for once, you didn't listen to me. We'd be dead now."

"Probably."

"I'm not very good at being vulnerable. And I'm certainly not good at apologizing. But I am sorry for being so difficult."

"You have your reasons."

"There are so many people in Washington I want to prove wrong. People who think women can't have a high-powered career in that city. They're mistaken. And it's time they learned that."

"I agree. But I also disagree. With something you said yesterday."

"What?"

"Friends are important. Feelings are important. Not everyone's out to hurt you. I'm not."

Grace looked up into Kay's eyes and frowned. "Are you making a pass at me, Miss Westmore?"

Kay laughed. "No. I just thought maybe we could be friends."

Grace poked Kay's shoulder. "What's so funny? You don't find me attractive?"

"I find you very attractive. But I don't think we're well-matched."

Grace sighed heavily. "No, you're right. Somehow I think I'm destined to continue my disastrous love relationships with men. I have my father to thank for that."

"You haven't met the right person yet."

"What about you? Have you met the right person?"

Kay shivered. It was Grace's turn to rub Kay's shoulders. "I don't know. If I have, I've probably lost her."

"If that's true, I'm sorry."

"Are you?"

"Yes. I am."

"At least I have a friend to feel sorry with."

Grace smiled. "Yeah, well, not if we freeze to death in this Alaskan ice pit."

Kay pulled the top of the sleeping bag over their heads. "Just stick close to me. And keep thinking warm thoughts."

"Oh, terrific. Something I've never been good at."

"You're learning."

CHAPTER NINE

Kay and Grace rode slowly up the hill to what was left of Dietrich Camp, once a thriving area during pipeline construction. Only four or five outbuildings remained — several of them dilapidated. Through a haze of fatigue Kay saw Russell's helicopter. Simultaneously, the door to the largest building opened. Out ran Russell and Lori, nearly frantic. Kay and Grace were three days behind schedule.

An hour later the helicopter landed at the old Chandalar Camp about twenty miles north of Dietrich

Camp. Chandalar Camp had been brought to life specifically for the project — with refurbished and heated outbuildings, including sleeping accommodations for all the teams. Kay felt slightly rejuvenated. They were more than halfway to Prudhoe Bay and the end of their nightmare.

Two hot meals and ten hours of sleep later, Kay walked toward the main building for the project update meeting Grace had termed "mandatory." Grace was standing at the front of the room staring at the rows of wooden benches where the team members sat staring back. Kay was seated next to Lori who put her arm around Kay's shoulder and gave her a quick hug.

"How're you feeling?"

"Fine, thanks."

Grace crossed her arms, pacing as she talked. Her demeanor had visibly softened and her words seemed genuinely sincere. "We've been out here for three weeks now. You've all done a great job — in spite of the weather, in spite of everything." She did a quarter turn toward the group and smiled. "So far, our efforts have shown that the pipeline's in good condition. I don't know what the last hundred and thirty miles will reveal, but I want to thank every one of you for your dedication and commitment to this effort."

Russell ambled toward the middle of the room and set a box on the table behind Grace.

"This box contains briefings and instructions for the last half of this inspection project. There's a copy for each member of each team," Grace said. "Take the one with your name on it and study it tonight. Report to your assigned teams or specific tasks tomorrow morning at six a.m. sharp. That's all for now."

At precisely 6:00 the next morning, Kay and Lori set out by snowmobile to check the line between the Chandalar and Antigun Camps. Antigun Camp was located near the Antigun Pass and continental divide, the high point of the pipeline route at 4,800 feet. By this time, Kay was used to the inspection monotony. She and Lori worked as a team — Lori keeping track of the weld numbers and results, Kay conducting the visual inspections.

Five hours into their assignment, day broke along the horizon in pinks and vibrant golds. Daylight, as short as it was, brought back a kind of normalcy to life that Kay missed. She and Lori stopped to eat a light lunch. They laid out a tarp underneath the line, sat down and fired up the portable stove. Kay was about to take her first sip of cocoa when she heard a truck approaching. In the distance she could barely make out a pick-up groaning up the Dalton Highway. Its tire chains clanked as it gripped for road, its engine straining with a violent hum. It was not a government vehicle.

As it drew closer, Lori said, "Oh, great. It's an Alyeska service truck."

"First one I've seen," Kay said. "They've been conspicuously absent for the last few miles."

"While you and Grace were en route to Wiseman,

we had some trouble back at Coldfoot. Some Alyeska crews stopped just west of the line, yelling some not-so-nice greetings. Later that same night, some of our equipment was sabotaged. And, we're minus two snowmobiles."

"No one told me about that."

"Grace knows. A few others. That's all. Grace swore us all to secrecy."

"Damn. Here they come."

The truck stopped. There were three men riding in the front cab. The back of the truck was covered with an Army-green tarp.

"Morning ladies," the driver said. He smiled through a heavy black beard. "What brings you up this way. Camping?"

Kay stood up. "Yeah. We're on vacation. Roughing it, you could say."

The man smiled again, pointing toward the snowmobile. "Nice machine."

"Thanks," Kay said warily.

Suddenly, the passenger side door opened. The two other men hopped out, coming around to the driver's side of the truck.

"Shit," Kay said under her breath. She hoped there wasn't going to be any trouble.

"For a minute, we thought you might be part of that government inspection team working its way up the line." It was a short, squat man talking, his dirty-blond hair framing the inside of his jacket hood. He spat on the ground, leaving a brown stain.

"Government?" Kay asked, trying to play dumb.

"Yeah. We work for the pipeline. The government doesn't think we do our jobs right." The man spat again, taking a few steps closer to Kay.

Lori got up and stood next to Kay. "Well, we wouldn't know anything about that. Paying my taxes is about all I can handle where the government's concerned."

The three men laughed.

"This is my first trip to Alaska," Kay said, throwing her hands up in the air to feign excitement. "I think the pipeline's the coolest thing I've ever seen. You guys keep up the good work."

"Where you from?" the driver asked.

"Spotswood, New Jersey," Kay lied.

The spitter spat again, his eyes squinting into the sun. "Never heard of it."

Kay shrugged. "Not much of a town."

"C'mon, guys," the driver said, waving the two men back to the truck. "Let's let these ladies get back to their vacationing."

Kay held her breath as they got back into the cab. The driver waved and she and Lori waved back. As they drove off, Kay couldn't help wondering what was in the back of the truck.

"I thought there was going to be trouble for sure," Lori said. "Think they believed us?"

"Don't know. C'mon, we've still got a lot of work to do before we get to Antigun."

They worked steadily for the next five hours until they finally reached Antigun. It was dark again, and Kay spotted a glow in the distance. It came from the window of the only remaining building in Antigun, other than some small storage sheds. Kay pulled the snowmobile into the shadows along the highway and cut off its engine. She focused her binoculars and, there, in plain view, parked right outside the weatherworn structure was the same Alyeska pickup she and Lori had seen earlier.

"Anything?" Lori asked, kneeling next to Kay.

"It's the same damned truck. Take a look."

Lori took the binoculars and scanned the entire camp. "That's it, all right. You've got something cooking up in that head of yours, Kay. What is it?"

"I want to see what's in that truck. I've got a feeling."

"What?"

"That we should check it out."

Just after midnight the building went dark. Kay and Lori moved outside the perimeter of the camp until they'd circled around to the north side, nearest the building. Slowly they made their way across open ground to the only cover — offered by the truck itself. The tarp covering the truck bed was tied on with a light but sturdy nylon rope. With her pocket knife, Kay was able to cut the rope and pull it through the metal eyelet anchors. She lifted the tarp's edge and crawled underneath. Her small Mag flashlight illuminated the darkness where she wasn't surprised to find the government's missing snowmobiles. There were other stolen supplies as well. But to Kay's greater horror there were about ten square packages wrapped in layers of see-through plastic. Some smaller cardboard boxes lay nearby. Heart pounding, Kay took one of each and got down out of the truck.

"What'd you find?"

"Let's get the hell out of here," Kay said, her

breath coming in gasps. "We've got to move our position into the wooded area to the west where we can keep an eye on these clowns but stay out of sight."

They set up camp — a quickly pitched tent under the cover of trees with a rise of rock to their west and north for wind block. Once inside, as Lori prepared two freeze-dried dinners, Kay examined the packages. It didn't take long to confirm her suspicions.

"Plastic explosives and blasting caps."

"Shit," Lori said. "What do you suppose they're up to?"

"Wish I knew. I've got to try and contact Russ. I just hope we're not out of range."

Kay went outside. She hoped, at their high elevation, the walkie-talkie would be able to find a channel back to Chandalar. The box crackled with static. Kay pushed the talk button, identified herself and waited for a response. None came. She tried again. Nothing. She stared at the rectangular box in disgust. She was beginning to take this personally. Then she heard a voice — faint, but surprisingly clear.

"G-two. Chandalar. Over."

"Kay Westmore at Antigun. Need to talk to Russell Bend. Emergency. Over."

"Stand by. Over."

While Kay waited, she peeked around the wall of rock that held them safely from view. The lights in the camp building were still out. Kay looked down at the plastic explosives she held in her hand. It can't be, she thought. Surely they weren't planning to blow up the pipeline.

"Russell Bend here. That you, Kay? Over."

"Russ, listen to me. Lori and I've stumbled onto something up here at Antigun. We're near the camp now." Kay went on to explain about the Alyeska crew, the stolen snowmobiles and other equipment — and the truckbed full of explosives.

"Stay right where you are, Kay. I'm going to leave now with a crew. I won't be able to fly the copter in. They'd hear it and be gone in no time. I'll take one of the trucks. You wait for me, understand?"

"As long as I can. But if they leave, I'm going to follow them. Over."

"Be careful, Kay. If the weather holds, I should be there in a couple of hours. You can reach me on channel five. Mobile One. It's a secured channel. Got it? Over."

"Got it. Hurry, Russ. Over and out."

Lori volunteered to take the first watch. The last Kay saw she was huddled on the hilltop smoking a cigarette, wrapped in her sleeping bag to keep warm. Kay quickly drifted into a restless sleep. About an hour and a half later, Lori woke her.

"Kay, something's up. The lights are on, and they're all moving around like they're getting ready to leave."

"Shit!" Kay checked her watch. Russ wouldn't get

there for another half-hour or more — depending on the condition of the highway, which Kay knew first-hand wasn't good. "Let's go get a closer look."

Kay grabbed her walkie-talkie and flashlight. They crept down the hillside toward the camp in small spurts, stopping every once in a while to listen for voices or activity. In the last of the trees before the clearing, they stooped, finally able to see the movements of two of the three men.

"Where's the third guy?" Kay asked.

"Haven't seen him yet."

"We've got to get closer."

"Kay, if they see us, we're dead."

"You go north." Kay pointed to the series of old sheds behind the main building. "Go to the end of the last shed. See if you can spot that other guy. I'm going to go south through the woods, across the clearing farther down and check out the pipeline."

"Shouldn't we wait for Russ?"

"There may not be time. Let's go."

Kay ran through the woods, slipping and sliding down snow-covered banks, finally reaching flat terrain. Through the trees, about two hundred yards ahead, lay the clearing and the road. When she came to the road, she stopped to listen. She heard a loud crack. Engines began revving in the distance. Suddenly, she saw them — two snowmobiles heading west away from the pipeline and the highway. She watched their headlights until she saw the machines slip into the woods, disappearing from view.

Kay dashed across the highway and headed for the pipeline. At this juncture, the pipeline was at its lowest elevation — two feet. There were no caribou or reindeer crossings here. No reason to elevate it to its maximum height of eight feet. Crouching, she ran along the line, checking every weld, looking for what she hoped she wouldn't find. And then she saw it. A red glow flashing in the darkness. She ran toward the flashing light and slid beneath the line. The flashing was the digital glow of a detonator affixed to a slab of plastic explosives. The detonator's timer was counting down and read fourteen minutes and fifty-three seconds. There were wires and a red button. The pack of explosives had been affixed to a weld. When the pipe blew, the oil would blow — across the plain and into the earth at the rate of 15,000 barrels per hour.

Kay pressed the button on her walkie-talkie. "Mobile One. Come in. Emergency. Mobile One, do you read?"

"Mobile One. I read you. Over."

"Russ, I've found a bomb — on the line and set to detonate in less than fourteen minutes."

"Christ! Listen, Kay. What does it look like? You've got to describe it to me. Every detail. I'm still about fifteen minutes ETA."

Kay's heart practically leapt from her throat. Stay calm, she told herself. Calm. She examined the device carefully with her flashlight. "Plastic explosives attached to the pipe itself. Metal box with a digital timer. Two wires leading from detonator into explosives. Detonator has a red button."

"What color are the wires?"

"One black and one red from the top of the detonator. One green from the bottom."

"How are the wires attached?"

"To the detonator or the explosives?"

"Both."

Less then twelve minutes. "The green and red wires are looped through a steel rod that's been slipped into the pack of explosives. The green runs underneath the explosive pack. I can't tell how it's connected. The red and black wires are attached to the detonator with screws."

"Good work, Kay. Now listen to me, do exactly what I tell you. Okay?"

Kay took a deep breath. Russ was an explosives expert; he'd spent fifteen years in the Navy as a demolitions specialist. "I'm ready."

"What tools do you have?"

"None!"

"You'll need a knife and a screwdriver."

Kay felt a sudden pounding in her temples. She'd left her tool pack in the tent. There was no time to get it. Then she remembered her survival tool. It had a screwdriver and a knife. She fumbled for it in her back pocket. "It's okay, Russ. I've got a screwdriver and a knife."

"Good. Unscrew the red wire first. Slowly, carefully."

Ten minutes left. "Red wire first? Over."

"Correct. Over."

Kay's hands shook as she fit the screwdriver into the tiny head. Where was Lori? After about fifteen seconds the wire slipped away. Kay held her breath. Nothing happened. But the timer still counted down. Nine minutes and thirty seconds left. "Okay. It's disconnected. Now what?"

"The green wire's next. It's a back-up detonator

— probably to a blasting cap on the underside of the explosive pack."

"How do I disconnect what I can't see?"

"You've got to cut the wire. You've got a knife?"

"Yes. Over."

"Without disturbing the wire's connection to the bomb, cut the wire clean."

Less then nine minutes left. Kay thought about what Russ had just told her. A clean cut. She prayed the knife would be sharp enough. She switched from the screwdriver to the small blade. Carefully, she placed the knife behind the wire where it had the most slack. Using her other hand, she pinched the wire into a loop. With one swift jerk of her thumb, she cut through the wire. The timer still counted down.

"Now what?" she yelled into the walkie-talkie.

"Press the red button. Over."

"Press the red button? Over."

"Correct. Over."

Kay could feel the sweat running down her neck. She pushed the red button. The timer blinked to triple zeroes. "I think that's it, Russ."

"Good work, Kay!"

"I've got to check the rest of the line. There may be more detonators."

"Go!"

Kay ran along the line checking the top of the pipe as well as the underside. About three welds later, her heart sank. Another bomb.

"Russ, I've found another one." Kay read the timer. Seven minutes and counting. "Seven minutes!"

"Is it the same type of device?" the reply came.

Kay crawled underneath the line. She checked the bomb quickly, but carefully. It was the same. "Yes. Over."

"Repeat the same steps. I'll talk you through them again."

Kay relived the same terror with this bomb. When the timer had reached five minutes, she pushed the button and the digital display flashed to triple zeroes. Without wasting a second, Kay got up and ran down the line. *Please, God. No more.* Time was running out. She could feel it. Where was Lori? She needed help and she needed it badly.

When Kay saw the blinking timer of another bomb, she almost crumbled inside. She dove feet first and slid under the line. Three minutes. No time to call Russ. It was the same type of device. Again, she repeated the steps to disarm the bomb. With fifty-eight seconds left, she found herself looking at triple zeroes. She was up again and running. Russ was calling her on the walkie-talkie. No time to answer. She ran and stumbled — and ran some more. Then she saw it. A larger box. Blinking green, not red. She scrambled beneath the pipe. This one was different. More wires. Two packs of explosives. This must be the insurance bomb, Kay thought. She looked at the digital timer. Four minutes and counting.

"Russ! Russ! I've found another one. Less than four minutes to detonation. But this one's different."

Russ was on the walkie-talkie immediately. "I'm almost there, Kay! Hang in! Describe it to me."

Kay panicked. She didn't know where to start.

"Kay!"

"Yes. Yes." Kay quickly gathered herself with one deep breath. "Two packs of explosives. Both connected to the same detonator. From screws on the top side of the detonator, two green . . . no, blue wires and a single red wire leading to each explosive pack. Two wires running under each pack from the bottom side of the detonator. Both yellow. There's a red button on the face of the detonator and a black one on the left side."

Three minutes and twenty seconds.

"Okay, Kay. Listen up. Unscrew the two blue wires first. Doesn't matter what order. Over."

"Unscrew the blue wires? Over."

"Correct. Over."

Kay did as Russ instructed. Three minutes.

"Now, cut each yellow wire on the underside. Again, it doesn't matter which you cut first. Over."

"Cut each yellow wire on the underside? Over."

"Correct. Over."

Kay completed the second step. One minute and forty-five seconds."

"Ready. What next?"

"Go back to the top of the detonator. Unscrew the red wire. Over."

"Unscrew the red wire? Over."

"Correct."

Eyes riveted to the timer, Kay started to unscrew the red wire. Her hands were freezing. Then she dropped the screwdriver. She saw it hit her chest and slide down her right side into the snow. "Oh, my God!" Kay rolled over, frantically searching with her flashlight. *Please, God. Help me.* Suddenly, she saw something glisten. Quickly, she grabbed the tool and turned back to the detonator. Fifty-nine seconds and counting.

"Done, Russ! Thirty seconds left. Hurry!"

"Press the black button on the side. Over."

"Black button on side? Over."

"Correct!"

Kay pressed the black button. The timer was down to fifteen seconds.

"Done!"

"Press the red button! Over."

"Red button? Over."

"Yes!"

With the timer reading nine seconds, Kay pressed the red button. Triple zeroes. She jumped up and ran. If there were any more bombs, it was too late.

CHAPTER TEN

Russ skidded the truck to a stop in front of the camp's main building. He was out of the vehicle like a shot, yelling for Kay. She ran from the woods and into Russ's arms. She could feel his barrel-like chest heaving with anxiety.

"Kay, I honestly didn't think I'd ever see you again. Did we get all the bombs?"

"Nothing's blown up for the last five minutes."

"One of our crew's only a few minutes behind me. They're gonna check the entire line in this sector." He brushed the hair away from her eyes.

"You did good, Kay. Real good." Russ took a quick look around. "Where's Lori?"

"Don't know. We split up about an hour ago and I haven't seen her since."

"C'mon. We'll find her."

They ran toward the main building. The door had been left ajar. Inside, the room was strewn with remnants of the Alyeska crew's brief stay. Empty food containers, cigarette butts, tobacco juice stains, used up fuel tins, pieces of wire, solder and a few tools. They found everything but Lori.

"Don't touch anything, Kay. The FBI's gonna be in on this investigation. I called Grace from the truck and she's already contacted the Bureau."

They went back outside and followed the line of weather-battered equipment sheds until they ended near the edge of woods at the camp's northernmost point. At the last shed they turned right. Up against the dirty-gray building, barely visible in the shadows, they found Lori lying on her side. With a quick sweep of her flashlight, Kay saw the pool of blood seeping into the snow.

"Lori!" Kay knelt down and carefully turned her face up. She heard a faint moan.

"She's alive," Russ said, unclipping the walkie-talkie from his belt. "I'll get a copter in here right away."

As Russ's voice boomed into the radio, Kay held Lori's head.

She opened her eyes and smiled. "Kay — I must've fallen asleep on the job. Or did I?"

"Don't think so."

Lori coughed, her eyes blinking away the discomfort. "No. I bumped into one of them while they were leaving. They didn't take too kindly to that. I tried to run..."

"Where are you hurt?"

"In the back, I think. Can't seem to feel my legs."

"Listen, you better be quiet. Russ's calling for help. We'll have you out of here in no time."

"Sure could use a cigarette."

"Not a good idea."

Russ returned with some blankets. "Help's on the way, kid."

Lori cradled herself against Kay and closed her eyes. "I'm tired."

Kay's eyes burned, and she could feel a warm trickle of blood on her fingers.

Kay stayed with Lori until the helicopter arrived. As soon as it landed the pilot and two paramedics jumped out. So did Grace Perry. Five minutes later, Lori was air-lifted to the nearest trauma hospital in Fort Yukon. Russ and the back-up crew went to conduct the line inspection.

"What the hell happened here?" Grace asked, agitated. Her eyes were dark and glassy. It was clear she hadn't slept for many hours.

"You talked to Russ?" Kay asked.

"About the explosives, yes." Grace clutched the front of Kay's parka. "Thank God you're all right. What happened to Lori?"

For the next few minutes, Kay explained in detail what had happened. Grace's expression turned from fear to anger, then she started to pace, her eyes lit with rage. "This should never've happened. I just cannot believe it. What's the matter with Alyeska? Up to this point, their security's been excellent — so much so that it's been a pain in the ass. Checkpoints. Air patrols. Even harassment. I don't understand." Grace spun around, grabbing Kay's arm. "My God, Kay. To think you could've been killed. And Lori . . ."

"I know. I'm worried sick about her."

"Damn, there's something very strange about all this. If I could only put my finger on what it is."

"Grace, think about it. You're absolutely right. We've been scrutinized by Alyeska security ever since we hit the line. But what about here, near Antigun? Nothing! Not one security patrol along this two-mile stretch. That hasn't happened once in the six weeks we've been out here."

Grace looked at Kay with a calculating stare. The wheels upstairs were turning. Assimilating everything. "Something's wrong. Terribly wrong. And I'm going to find out what it is." She took Kay's hand. "I smell a rat, Kay. And it's got the smell of the D.C. sewers on it."

A week later the team finally reached Prudhoe Bay. Kay followed the caravan of snowmobiles into the town of Deadhorse. Grace called a meeting of all teams for that afternoon. She gave a report concerning Lori Kincaid's medical condition. Lori had been transferred to Georgetown University Hospital in D.C. She was stable and responding to treatment. Grace also reported on what had developed so far in the investigation of the attempted pipeline sabotage at Antigun.

"Federal investigators have told me that Alyeska

security was deliberately diverted to other locations on the line by a series of radio calls. As a result, a two-mile stretch at Antigun was left unwatched. This gave the saboteurs the opportunity to plant the explosives. We were fortunate that Miss Westmore and Miss Kincaid were conducting inspections in that sector. That's all we know right now. The investigation's ongoing."

After two full days of inspections in the Deadhorse area, Kay woke up groggily in her room at the Deadhorse Inn. It was a large enough establishment to finally have her own room and some much needed privacy. Kay struggled out of bed to take a shower. The hot shower made her even more tired. She threw on a robe and fell across the bed in an exhausted stupor.

The courtroom on her side was empty except for the first row where Alex and Pat sat. The maple benches on the other side of the courtroom, directly behind her sister and brother-in-law, were filled with distant family relations, friends and co-workers of both her sister and brother-in-law — along with many people she'd never seen before. Sitting in the witness chair beside the judge, Kay felt very much alone. She smiled at her father for reassurance and he bent his head in shame — and pain. Shame because he could no longer care for himself. Pain because of Kay's pain. He'd told Kay he hadn't wanted this courtroom scene, didn't want Kay to be hurt. He wanted Kay to handle his affairs but had been judged unable to decide for himself. So the court would decide at her father's expense. And, as Kay was about to find out, at her own.

Kay's questioning, at the hand of her sister's lawyer, had begun about a half-hour before. The thirty-something preppy lawyer, Raymond Collier, was one of her brother-in-law's best friends. His initial questions concerned Kay's relationship with her father, her sister and mother, plus questions about work and career plans.

There had been a brief recess and then her sister's lawyer slid out from behind the front table and approached, his hands punched into an expensive Italian suit. Collier swaggered and cleared his throat.

"Do you own your own home, Miss Westmore?"

"Yes."

"Do you live alone?"

"No."

"With whom do you reside?"

"A friend. Barbara Reynolds."

The tall, solidly built man turned toward the judge. "A *friend*?"

"Correct."

"Isn't it true that Barbara Reynolds is your lover and that you, Miss Westmore, are a lesbian?"

Kay's lawyer, Constance Steward, jumped from her seat. "Objection, your honor. This line of questioning is irrelevant. Miss Westmore's lifestyle has no bearing on her ability to make decisions concerning her father's welfare."

The judge leaned forward, his dark eyes flashing annoyance. "The attorneys will please approach the bench."

As the judge and attorneys exchanged words, Kay glared at her sister. There seemed to be no remorse in her eyes, no regret on her face. Her brother-in-law was smirking, clearly pleased with the new line of questioning.

Constance Steward returned to her chair. She did not look happy.

"Objection overruled," the judge said. "You may answer the question, Miss Westmore."

Kay concentrated, with all her will, on remaining steady. "That's correct," she said calmly. "We've been together for four years."

"So you acknowledge your homosexuality, Miss Westmore?"

"Yes."

"Is Miss Reynolds here today?" Collier asked, pointing toward the open courtroom.

"No. She's working."

"And prior to your relationship with Miss Reynolds, how many other lesbian affairs have you had?"

"Objection, your honor."

"Overruled. You may answer."

Kay was infuriated. "I don't remember," she snapped.

"You don't remember, Miss Westmore? Would you describe yourself as promiscuous then?"

"Of course not."

"Have you ever had several lovers at once?"

"No."

"Have you ever gone to bars to pick up other women?"

"Have you?" Kay asked sarcastically.

Collier laughed, his blond mustache twitching with delight. "Well, now, if I did, Miss Westmore, it would be considered normal, wouldn't it?"

Kay didn't respond. She glanced at her father. His head was buried in his hands. His shoulders were shaking with tears. Kay looked at her sister. "You're the one who's hurting Pop, Julia. Look at him."

"Objection. The witness wasn't asked to speak," Collier said.

"Miss Westmore, please confine your answers to Mr. Collier's questions," the judge instructed.

"Have you ever gone for any kind of counseling, Miss Westmore?"

Kay couldn't believe it. Her sister hadn't held anything back. "Yes."

"Was it voluntary?"

"Not exactly."

"Who sent you?"

"My mother."

"For what reason?"

"Because . . ." Kay stopped. She felt so betrayed.

"We're waiting, Miss Westmore."

"My mother didn't agree with my lifestyle."

There was a low murmur throughout the courtroom.

"What about your father?"

"My father's always accepted me for who I am."

"Did he object to the idea of counseling?"

"It wasn't his idea."

"That wasn't my question, Miss Westmore. I

asked if your father objected to your mother's recommendation that you obtain the services of a professional counselor?"

Kay bowed her head. "No."

Collier turned on his heels. "That's all, Miss Westmore. I have nothing further."

Two days later, the judge made his decision. Kay's father was to live with Jack and Julia. They were to be his legal guardians — in control of all his finances and the home care he needed. That arrangement lasted less than a year. As soon as Jack had found a way to "hide" her father's money in his own investments and real estate deals, they put Kay's father in the county home.

Kay woke up with a start. Grace was sitting on the edge of her bed.

"Something tells me you weren't having a very nice dream."

"No, I wasn't."

Grace brushed the damp hair from Kay's face. "You should be dreaming about that beautiful young lady waiting for you back in Fairbanks. Hopefully, you'll see her soon."

"Maybe. I don't know."

"Well, I'm sorry to bother you, Kay. God knows, we're all exhausted. But Russ and I need your help. Do you mind?"

Kay smiled. Weeks ago, she would have minded any request from Grace Perry. Thankfully, that had changed.

"No, I don't mind."

* * * * *

The laptop computer sitting in front of Russ beeped again. "Shit! What the hell did they send us?"

Kay sat down next to him. The stress of the trip was beginning to take its toll on everyone. She tried a few keystrokes of her own and finally the hard drive began to rumble, indicating that the transferred files were being loaded. "I think we're in business now."

Grace had asked Russ and Kay to obtain past pipeline inspection data through Donnelly and the Fairbanks office. The old data was to be compared with the recent inspection stats so a comparison could be made for final reporting.

A few minutes passed and then Russell imported the old data into the new database file. "There. Now we can set up a new spreadsheet."

Suddenly, the hard drive started to flutter again and the spreadsheet screen flashed "wait" in the upper right corner. "Now what?" Kay asked.

"Who the hell knows. Donnelly must've gotten this stuff from the night-shift janitors at Interior. Whoever created this disk really skunked it up."

"Well, it loaded a second file into the database. Scroll down to see if anything's there."

Russ ran through the spreadsheet screen page by page. He couldn't find anything.

"That's odd," Kay said.

For hours the two worked integrating the data. By the end of the afternoon, after a big lunch and countless cups of coffee, they still weren't finished.

More data comparisons had to be made, as well as all the charting and graphing.

"I need a break, Russ. Let's save this thing, back it up and start fresh tomorrow."

"I'm with ya. My eyes are starting to weird out on me. All the numbers look the same."

Russ did as Kay suggested and closed the file. Immediately, the screen flashed out to the hard drive directories. Russ was about to exit the program when Kay stopped him.

"Russ, look. There's a new directory here." Kay pointed to the screen. "PSABCRE. What's that?"

"Beats me. Let's open it and find out."

Kay watched as Russell opened the directory. There was only one file listed: GOEAD.DEC. Russell imported it into the spreadsheet. The screen filled with unintelligible characters and a combination of letters and numbers.

"It's some kind of programming language. PASCAL, I think."

"What's it mean?"

"Hell, I don't know. Let me see that disk."

Kay gave him the data disk that Donnelly's secretary had sent. It was marked "Pipeline Inspection Data, 1990–1995." The last five years, just as Grace had requested.

Russell scratched his head. "This must be a word processing file. The spreadsheet software can't read it."

"Try importing it into WordPerfect."

"Do we have that on here?"

"Uh huh. I'll do it."

Kay's hands sped over the keys. She loaded Word-Perfect and called up the errant directory. She selected the lone file and imported it into the word processing package. This time, there were unintelligible characters, but they had a different look to them. A kind of shorthand, Kay thought.

"This is gibberish, too," Russ said.

"Sure looks like it."

She studied the screen. There was a group of letters amidst all the jumble that intrigued her. TO/EAD. DECINSPC. APPRVDCRE/EXx4 . . . 3/ SECTS. GO/ANTI.SLOP.FRANK. 12BGN09.

"What does that look like to you, Russ?"

"Nothing. A bunch of garbage."

"Maybe not. TO EAD. This is Donnelly's file, right?"

"Right."

"Edward Andrew Donnelly. TO EAD."

"So, you're saying this is a message to Donnelly?"

"Yeah. DECINSPC. December inspection?"

Russ sat up straight. "I think you've got something here, Kay."

All night and into the next morning, they slaved over this one section of type. When Russ finally figured out what GO/ANTI.SLOP.FRANK meant, it started to come together. Both Kay and Russ looked at each other in disbelief.

"I think what we've got here, Russ — and stop me if you think I'm wrong — is an approval from CRE, Charles Robert Eagleton, to Donnelly to go ahead with the planting of explosives along the line."

"Exactly. Go ANTI. It's a go for Antigun — where we defused the first batch of explosives. SLOP must mean the Slope Mountain Camp and FRANK the

Franklin Bluffs Camp. Three SECTS means those three sectors. I still don't know what EXx four means."

For a few minutes both Kay and Russ were quiet. Then Kay snapped her fingers.

"What if it means four explosive charges per sector?"

"Christ! Kay, we've got to talk to Grace right away. I assume this other thing means to begin on December ninth. That's the day they set the explosives at Antigun. Suppose they're still planning to hit Slope Mountain and Franklin Bluffs?"

"Let's go."

A week later, Kay sat in the restaurant down the street from the inn having a cup of coffee and reading a week-old newspaper. Out of the corner of her eye she saw Grace Perry approach her table.

"Can we talk, Kay?"

"Of course." Kay folded the newspaper and threw it on the chair next to her.

Grace smiled and sat down across from Kay. "Time to say good-bye, at least for a while. I need to get back to Washington."

"Something urgent?"

"Got a call this morning. There's some new information about the investigation. I'm meeting with the FBI as soon as I get back."

"Good luck."

"Thanks, Kay. Here's a copy of the final inspection report. I thought you might like to take a look at it. And just so you know, security's been beefed up in the Slope Mountain and Franklin Bluffs sectors. I don't think anything will happen now. Our friends have been exposed."

"It's really unbelievable."

"You haven't hung around Washington long enough. After sloshing through the political cesspool as long as I have, nothing surprises me anymore."

"Guess not."

"Listen, Kay. There's something I've been wanting to say. Remember back in the conference room in Fairbanks? When I asked about that young lady I saw you with at the university?"

"I remember."

"You made a joke about how I'd probably have her investigated or something."

"Did you?"

Grace chuckled. "Of course not. The reason I asked about her was — well, when I saw you two together, I saw something special, Kay. I know that sounds trite and silly." Grace blushed. "Oh, what am I trying to say, here?" She paused. "It was the way she looked at you, Kay. I see it now and think, my God, Kay's lucky. She's found someone who really loves her — and that's more than I've ever been able to do. Unfortunately, I've dedicated most of life to my job. But a job doesn't love you back."

Kay rested her hand on Grace's arm. "Thank you. It means a lot to me that you cared enough to say something."

Grace quickly gathered her coat and a pile of bound reports. "Well, I've got to go. I'm putting you in charge while I'm gone. To wrap things up, if you don't mind."

"Not at all."

Grace got up and Kay helped her with her coat. She pulled it up over Grace's shoulders and Grace immediately turned around. "Now, I've got one last assignment for you, Miss Westmore."

Kay smiled. "Fire away, Grace."

"Out on the line, down by the landing area, Russ's waiting for you. An important passenger's been flown in." Grace looked at her watch. "I want you down there in five minutes." Picking up her briefcase, Grace backed away. "This person's strictly VIP, Kay. So get going."

"I'm on my way."

"You'll be hearing from me."

"I hope so."

Suddenly, with a brisk stride, Grace Perry disappeared from view.

Kay stood for a few moments in an awkward daze. Two months ago, she never would've believed it possible. She was going to miss Grace Perry. Picking up her copy of the bound report, Kay quickly leafed through its more than two hundred pages. The same report the President would review. Its basic summary concluded that the pipeline was structurally sound all along its 800-mile route from Valdez to Prudhoe Bay. The line was environmentally safe — built to the high standards that the state of Alaska and the people of Alaska had demanded from the onset of construction in 1975.

The sun was coming up, shining orange-red on the pipeline's surface. The reflection gave the illusion of fire — as though the long metal structure was ablaze against the shadow-cast snow. It could have been, Kay thought. At Antigun.

Kay approached the pipeline and stopped for a moment. The past two months seemed to flash like an old-time movie in her mind. Some of the images were already starting to fade. Others seemed blurred or disjointed, others struck terror into her heart. She had followed the line like a path to something — or to some end. But whatever that ending was, she knew it hadn't happened yet. It was still out there, waiting for her.

Reluctantly, she turned and headed north toward the landing pad. In the distance, Kay could barely make out the bulky figure of Russ, unloading some supplies from the helicopter's rear compartment. Standing next to him was a much smaller figure in a dark hooded parka. Kay kept walking, trudging along the path that mimicked the line. By force of habit, she mentally inspected these few remaining pipeline sections. No visible damage.

Suddenly, the helicopter landing area was only a few feet away. And there, at the end of the line, near the valves and pumps and high-rise-like structures that pulled oil from earth, Kay finally found what she'd really been looking for. Not weld defects or oil leaks or saboteurs. Not anything to do with the job or the people or the pipeline. She found what she'd left behind. And in that instant, she realized that what she'd left behind was what really mattered. Just as Grace had tried to tell her only a few minutes before.

Russ smiled and moved away, leaving them alone. Kay said a silent prayer that what she had found had also found her.

"Hiya, Kay."

"You flew all this way to see me?"

Stef pulled her hood back. Her blond hair swirled in the wind. "I missed you so much, Kay. I tried it your way. No commitment. I even went out a few times while you were gone. But . . ."

"But what?"

"I love you, Kay. That's the way it is. I know I'm young and it sounds so simple — especially after all you've been through with Barb and your family. But that's how it is for me. I came to find out what you want. And if I'm a part of what you want."

Kay took a few steps closer. It was like taking a few steps closer to life — away from the past and all that was gone and finally finished. "I'm sorry for what I've put you through. And if you can forgive me, and put up with whatever may still be ahead of us, I'd be a fool not to say that you're everything I want, Stef. Everything."

Stef threw her arms around Kay and held her tightly. Kay remembered the first time they'd danced — how perfectly they had fit together. It was still true.

"I love you, Stef." It was the first time she'd said the words. It finally felt right to say them.

"I love you too."

CHAPTER ELEVEN

Kay approached him quietly from behind. He was in the recreational room watching television. When she reached his wheelchair, she wrapped her arms around his neck. "Hey, Pop. Did you miss me?"

Kay circled the chair to face him. His eyes brightened and he tried to smile. Taking his hand, she knelt in front of him. "I brought your Christmas presents. Sorry they're a little late."

"You're my Christmas present," he said.

"I missed you, Pop."

"Missed you. No good company. No sneaking out."

Kay laughed. "C'mon, let's go open some packages."

Kay wheeled her father to his room. She helped him open his gifts. New slippers. Two flannel shirts. A new pair of slacks. After shave and soap-on-a-rope.

Her father held up one of the shirts. "I want to put this on."

"No problem. I'll help you." Kay unfolded the shirt, removing the straight pins and cardboard. As she helped him change, she told him about the trip. What had happened along the pipeline. The long days, terrible weather. The explosives she'd had to defuse. He seemed to study her with fascination — or maybe disbelief. She didn't know which.

"Kay, what you did. It was dangerous."

"Yes. It was."

"But they picked you because you're good."

"That's why they picked all of us."

"You did something important. For our country." Her father's head drooped. "For this beautiful state of ours." With the balls of his feet, he swung his wheelchair around. "That I don't see anymore . . . except through your eyes." He pointed toward the window. "If it weren't for you . . . that's all I'd ever see."

Kay looked out the window. It was a view of the annex roof, tar-topped with several large steel boxes that provided heat to the complex. Steam rose from a rusted vent like a ghost from a graveyard. Cars pulled into an adjacent parking lot. To the left were two solitary lines of trees cut through by the road.

Kay put her hands on top of her father's shoulders. "I'm thinking of buying a house, Pop. Would you want to come and live with me?"

"Julia wouldn't let me."

"She and Jack got what they wanted. There's not a whole lot left they can take from us, Pop. Is there?"

"No. I didn't care so much about the money. But what they did to you . . ."

"It's over, Pop. And it's time you came home."

The river shone like glitter in the sun — running cool through the valley on this late-spring day. Across the river, the open plain faded into the hills, still brown but budding. And in the far distance, the snow-capped peaks jutted into the blue sky, cutting a place for themselves into the heavens.

Kay sat under the enormous spruce on a picnic blanket. In her lap, Stef's head rested — eyes closed, hands wrapped around Kay's forearm. The eyes suddenly opened, peering up at Kay with a studied gaze.

"Did I fall asleep?"

"You did."

"It was all that food. You musn't let me get fat, Kay."

"Why? I'd love you anyway."

"You would?"

"Of course." Kay ran her fingers through Stef's windblown hair. "There'd be more to love and I'd be all the more exhausted."

"Am I that much trouble?"

Kay laughed. "This kind of trouble I should've had long ago. I'm just glad you hung in and waited for me to come to my senses."

"It was worth the wait."

"Was it? You should've taken off running the first night Barb showed up at the bar."

"Barb was sick, Kay. Now she's in that hospital. I feel sorry for her. Don't you?"

"Yes."

Stef put her arms around Kay's neck. "I can't believe it's been exactly a year since we first met."

"It was about this time, too. I remember being on that dock down below. And then I heard your voice and turned. After all the pain with Barb I thought I'd never feel it again."

"What?"

"Alive. Aware of everything. Especially you." Kay pushed Stef backward onto the blanket. "But I couldn't do what I really wanted to do then — that first day."

"Tell me what you wanted to do."

"Kiss you. Just once. To see if you were for real."

"Why don't you kiss me now?"

As Kay kissed Stef, like she'd wanted to that very first day, the wind kicked up and blew the blanket over top of them. And under the blanket, beneath the shelter of that soaring spruce, Stef showed Kay just how real she was.

EPILOGUE

Five months after completing the pipeline inspection, Kay stood in the receiving line trying to come to grips with the events leading to this time and place. To her left, in the section reserved for family, Stef, in a mint-green sweater and black slacks, gave her the thumbs up sign. In front of Stef was Kay's father, sitting proudly in his wheelchair in the only suit and tie he owned. To Kay's right, Russ stood — not in a tuxedo but in a slate-gray suit, maroon tie and a pair of stiff black dress shoes that clearly hurt when he walked. To his right, Lori

Kincaid also sat in a wheelchair. She was still recovering from the gunshot wound. A 22-caliber bullet lay half an inch from her spinal cord. Still, there was real hope that she would someday walk again.

Across from them all, Grace Perry stood amidst a sea of Washington dignitaries that included senators, members of Congress, cabinet officials and personal aides to the President. In front of Grace, Maria was smiling proudly. Grace Perry was now Secretary Perry. She had recently been confirmed as the new Secretary of the Interior following the completed investigation of the attempted sabotage to the Trans-Alaska Pipeline near Antigun. The investigation had revealed that Acting Secretary of the Interior, Charles Eagleton, had hired the saboteurs, through several levels of intermediaries, including Edward Donnelly, to damage a pipeline that was structurally healthy and sound. After being briefed by Grace Perry halfway through the investigation, Eagleton felt the Interior post slipping from his grasp. Through sabotage, he had hoped to bolster his claims that the pipeline was unsafe — putting a lock on his bid to join the President's cabinet. The discovery of the conspiracy was a personal blow to the Vice President, who knew nothing of the Acting Secretary's plan. Eagleton had been a close friend and advisor. Now he was on his way to prison — paving the way for Grace.

Donnelly was on his way to prison, too. He had been lured by Eagleton and the promise of a significant position within the administration.

A little over eight weeks ago, while sitting in her downtown Fairbanks office, Kay had been startled by a knock on her door. It was after five and most everyone had left for the day.

"Door's open. C'mon in."

In walked Grace Perry. She was wearing a full-length black leather coat that held her long auburn hair underneath its collar. Her deep earthen eyes shone with the happiness of surprising Kay.

"Happy to see me?"

"My God, yes! What brings you to Fairbanks?"

"Can you have dinner?"

Kay stammered. "Uh, well . . . I suppose so."

Grace laughed. "Why don't you call that young lady of yours and tell her you're having dinner with an old friend who's got a lot of clout in Washington and may be your new boss. I think that ought to settle things."

Kay made the phone call.

The restaurant was one of Kay's favorites. An old renovated hotel with candlelit rooms and great food, including the best salmon in Alaska. And that's what they ordered, savoring every bite. In between courses, Grace filled Kay in on the results of the pipeline investigation, Eagleton and Donnelly's involvement and her own nomination as Secretary of the Interior. The nomination would come before the Senate for a vote next week. Confirmation seemed assured.

"I'm happy for you, Grace. You deserve it. Congratulations."

"Thank you, Kay. I couldn't have done it without your help." Grace took a sip of wine. "How's that young lady of yours?"

"Great. We bought a house. My dad's living with us too."

"How lovely."

"May I ask you a personal question?"

"Of course, Kay."

"Your daughter, Maria. Have you seen her?"

Grace's eyes lit up. "Yes. I worked out a new visitation schedule with Vince. I see her every other weekend now."

"Glad to hear it." Kay pushed her plate away.

"Well, surprise. When you visit Washington next month, you'll get a chance to meet her." Grace reached down and took an envelope from her briefcase.

The envelope was made out to Kay in elegant script. On the back was the Presidential seal. Kay looked at Grace, totally confused.

"Well, go ahead and open it."

Kay opened the envelope. Inside, under delicate tissue paper, was the letterhead of the President. It was an announcement that read:

The President of the United States
on the Third Day of May
in the Year Nineteen Hundred and Ninety-Six
at Two O'clock p.m.
will Present the Presidential Medal of Freedom
to
Kay Lynn Westmore
on
Behalf of the People of the United States of America
for
Significant Contribution Made to the National
Interest.

"I nominated you, Kay. Along with Russell and Lori. You'll all be there — and deservedly so. The

President wants the country to know that three Interior employees were willing to risk their lives for national and environmental security. Now it's my turn to say congratulations."

"Grace, I don't know what to say. Thank you."

"I hope it makes up a little bit for my treatment of you when we first met. Not that you wouldn't have been nominated anyway. I just filled out the paperwork."

"We're friends, Grace. That's where we've come. Over a rough road maybe. But we got here in spite of it all."

"And soon, it'll be just like old times, Kay. The position of National Park Service, Regional Director, Alaska, is vacant thanks to Donnelly and Eagleton. It's all yours, Kay. You're the best person for the job. You'll be working for me again. Won't that be wonderful?"

Kay raised her eyebrows.

Grace chuckled. "Don't worry. My office is at least two thousand miles away."

"Well, maybe I can handle it then." Kay held up her glass. "Here's to your success."

"Our success."

The President stood directly before Kay; he was over six feet tall with piercing blue eyes and distinguished gray hair. His youthful face was already lined with the difficulties he'd faced during his first four-year term. In his hand was the Presidential Medal of Freedom. The President had already presented medals to Lori Kincaid and Russell Bend.

"Miss Westmore, it's an honor to present you with The Medal of Freedom on behalf of your country," he said, pinning it to her collar. Cameras flashed, people clapped and the President grasped her hand firmly. "For risking your life to ensure our country's environmental protection and preserve our energy independence, I am deeply grateful."

"Thank you, sir. For this great honor. Thank you."

The President nodded and shook her hand again. Then there was bedlam as a line of people, including Grace Perry, gathered to congratulate Kay, Russell and Lori.

A few minutes later, the President asked to meet their families. Kay introduced the President to Stef and then to her father.

The President bent to shake her father's hand. "Mr. Westmore, you must be extremely proud of your daughter."

Kay's father struggled to meet the President's eyes. In a clear and forceful voice he answered, "Yes, I am. Always have been."

LOVE ON THE LINE by Laura DeHart Young. 176 pp. Will Stef win Kay's heart? ISBN 1-56280-162-7 $11.95

DEVIL'S LEG CROSSING by Kaye Davis. 192 pp. 1st Maris Middleton mystery. ISBN 1-56280-158-9 11.95

COSTA BRAVA by Marta Balletbo Coll. 144 pp. Read the book, see the movie! ISBN 1-56280-153-8 11.95

MEETING MAGDALENE & OTHER STORIES by Marilyn Freeman. 144 pp. Read the book, see the movie! ISBN 1-56280-170-8 11.95

SECOND FIDDLE by Kate Calloway. 208 pp. P.I. Cassidy James' second case. ISBN 1-56280-169-6 11.95

LAUREL by Isabel Miller. 128 pp. By the author of the beloved *Patience and Sarah*. ISBN 1-56280-146-5 10.95

LOVE OR MONEY by Jackie Calhoun. 240 pp. The romance of real life. ISBN 1-56280-147-3 10.95

SMOKE AND MIRRORS by Pat Welch. 224 pp. 5th Helen Black Mystery. ISBN 1-56280-143-0 10.95

DANCING IN THE DARK edited by Barbara Grier & Christine Cassidy. 272 pp. Erotic love stories by Naiad Press authors. ISBN 1-56280-144-9 14.95

TIME AND TIME AGAIN by Catherine Ennis. 176 pp. Passionate love affair. ISBN 1-56280-145-7 10.95

PAXTON COURT by Diane Salvatore. 256 pp. Erotic and wickedly funny contemporary tale about the business of learning to live together. ISBN 1-56280-114-7 10.95

INNER CIRCLE by Claire McNab. 208 pp. 8th Carol Ashton Mystery. ISBN 1-56280-135-X 10.95

LESBIAN SEX: AN ORAL HISTORY by Susan Johnson. 240 pp. Need we say more? ISBN 1-56280-142-2 14.95

BABY, IT'S COLD by Jaye Maiman. 256 pp. 5th Robin Miller
Mystery.   ISBN 1-56280-141-4   19.95

WILD THINGS by Karin Kallmaker. 240 pp. By the undisputed
mistress of lesbian romance.   ISBN 1-56280-139-2   10.95

THE GIRL NEXT DOOR by Mindy Kaplan. 208 pp. Just what
you'd expect.   ISBN 1-56280-140-6   10.95

NOW AND THEN by Penny Hayes. 240 pp. Romance on the
westward journey.   ISBN 1-56280-121-X   10.95

HEART ON FIRE by Diana Simmonds. 176 pp. The romantic and
erotic rival of *Curious Wine.*   ISBN 1-56280-152-X   10.95

DEATH AT LAVENDER BAY by Lauren Wright Douglas. 208 pp.
1st Allison O'Neil Mystery.   ISBN 1-56280-085-X   10.95

YES I SAID YES I WILL by Judith McDaniel. 272 pp. Hot
romance by famous author.   ISBN 1-56280-138-4   10.95

FORBIDDEN FIRES by Margaret C. Anderson. Edited by Mathilda
Hills. 176 pp. Famous author's "unpublished" Lesbian romance.
                                            ISBN 1-56280-123-6   21.95

SIDE TRACKS by Teresa Stores. 160 pp. Gender-bending
Lesbians on the road.   ISBN 1-56280-122-8   10.95

HOODED MURDER by Annette Van Dyke. 176 pp. 1st Jessie
Batelle Mystery.   ISBN 1-56280-134-1   10.95

WILDWOOD FLOWERS by Julia Watts. 208 pp. Hilarious and
heart-warming tale of true love.   ISBN 1-56280-127-9   10.95

NEVER SAY NEVER by Linda Hill. 224 pp. Rule #1: Never get involved
with . . .   ISBN 1-56280-126-0   10.95

THE SEARCH by Melanie McAllester. 240 pp. Exciting top cop
Tenny Mendoza case.   ISBN 1-56280-150-3   10.95

THE WISH LIST by Saxon Bennett. 192 pp. Romance through
the years.   ISBN 1-56280-125-2   10.95

FIRST IMPRESSIONS by Kate Calloway. 208 pp. P.I. Cassidy
James' first case.   ISBN 1-56280-133-3   10.95

OUT OF THE NIGHT by Kris Bruyer. 192 pp. Spine-tingling
thriller.   ISBN 1-56280-120-1   10.95

NORTHERN BLUE by Tracey Richardson. 224 pp. Police recruits
Miki & Miranda — passion in the line of fire. ISBN 1-56280-118-X   10.95

LOVE'S HARVEST by Peggy J. Herring. 176 pp. by the author of
Once More With Feeling.   ISBN 1-56280-117-1   10.95

THE COLOR OF WINTER by Lisa Shapiro. 208 pp. Romantic
love beyond your wildest dreams.   ISBN 1-56280-116-3   10.95

FAMILY SECRETS by Laura DeHart Young. 208 pp. Enthralling
romance and suspense.   ISBN 1-56280-119-8   10.95

INLAND PASSAGE by Jane Rule. 288 pp. Tales exploring conventional & unconventional relationships.　　ISBN 0-930044-56-8　　10.95

DOUBLE BLUFF by Claire McNab. 208 pp. 7th Carol Ashton Mystery.　　ISBN 1-56280-096-5　　10.95

BAR GIRLS by Lauran Hoffman. 176 pp. See the movie, read the book!　　ISBN 1-56280-115-5　　10.95

THE FIRST TIME EVER edited by Barbara Grier & Christine Cassidy. 272 pp. Love stories by Naiad Press authors.
　　ISBN 1-56280-086-8　　14.95

MISS PETTIBONE AND MISS McGRAW by Brenda Weathers. 208 pp. A charming ghostly love story.　　ISBN 1-56280-151-1　　10.95

CHANGES by Jackie Calhoun. 208 pp. Involved romance and relationships.　　ISBN 1-56280-083-3　　10.95

FAIR PLAY by Rose Beecham. 256 pp. 3rd Amanda Valentine Mystery.　　ISBN 1-56280-081-7　　10.95

PAYBACK by Celia Cohen. 176 pp. A gripping thriller of romance, revenge and betrayal.　　ISBN 1-56280-084-1　　10.95

THE BEACH AFFAIR by Barbara Johnson. 224 pp. Sizzling summer romance/mystery/intrigue.　　ISBN 1-56280-090-6　　10.95

GETTING THERE by Robbi Sommers. 192 pp. Nobody does it like Robbi!　　ISBN 1-56280-099-X　　10.95

FINAL CUT by Lisa Haddock. 208 pp. 2nd Carmen Ramirez Mystery.　　ISBN 1-56280-088-4　　10.95

FLASHPOINT by Katherine V. Forrest. 256 pp. A Lesbian blockbuster!　　ISBN 1-56280-079-5　　10.95

CLAIRE OF THE MOON by Nicole Conn. Audio Book —Read by Marianne Hyatt.　　ISBN 1-56280-113-9　　16.95

FOR LOVE AND FOR LIFE: INTIMATE PORTRAITS OF LESBIAN COUPLES by Susan Johnson. 224 pp.
　　ISBN 1-56280-091-4　　14.95

DEVOTION by Mindy Kaplan. 192 pp. See the movie — read the book!　　ISBN 1-56280-093-0　　10.95

SOMEONE TO WATCH by Jaye Maiman. 272 pp. 4th Robin Miller Mystery.　　ISBN 1-56280-095-7　　10.95

GREENER THAN GRASS by Jennifer Fulton. 208 pp. A young woman — a stranger in her bed.　　ISBN 1-56280-092-2　　10.95

These are just a few of the many Naiad Press titles — we are the oldest and largest lesbian/feminist publishing company in the world. We also offer an enormous selection of lesbian video products. Please request a complete catalog. We offer personal service; we encourage and welcome direct mail orders from individuals who have limited access to bookstores carrying our publications.